Knot what I want for Christmas

Hannah Haze

Foreword

This book is a 'why choose' omegaverse romance with one female omega main character and three male alphas who are part of a pack.

The story is set in a ranch during winter and while I've tried to make this story realistic to the setting, sometimes the realism has to bend for "story and romance" reasons!

For more detailed content warnings, please visit my website.

If you spot any typos in this book, please drop me a line so I can make it right: hannahhazewrites@gmail.com (Or just drop me an email anyway. I love to chat!).

A very happy holidays to you all — may all your festive wishes come true and may you be blessed with many earth-shattering kisses beneath the mistletoe!

Chapter One

H ollie

I push the rickety luggage trolley through the airport arrivals, dodging tourists, swerving small children, and struggling to keep the sucker on the straight and narrow.

Why do I always pick the trolley with the freaky wheel? I mean, this time I even inspected all four, and they looked absolutely fine until I started pushing. The thing keeps veering to the left no matter how hard I push it in the opposite direction.

Finally, I make it through the big airport exit doors, out into the Rocky Mountain air and...

It's snowing!

It's actually snowing!

Snowflakes swirling in the air, everything covered in a thick icing of white, powdery dust. It's like I've just stepped straight into a snow globe. And it whips my breath right away.

Snow. I haven't seen snow since... When was it? Some vacation with Mom when I was a kid, probably seven or eight, and that snow was sludgy and wet and dirty. Now this is real snow. Pretty, sparkling Christmas snow.

I can't help but laugh, reaching out my hand to let the snowflakes land in my palm. When I left Rockview five hours ago, it was in the 70s and blazing hot sunshine. Now I'm here in the Rockies and it's snowing.

I fling my arms out wide, spin around, and then I do what any other sensible 30-year-old woman would do who hasn't seen snow since she was seven years old. I stick out my tongue and try to catch one of those flakes in my mouth.

"Hey!" a deep, growly voice says from beside me, making me jump out of my skin, and nearly bite my tongue in half.

I stuff my tongue straight back in my mouth, flip my head to the side, and try my best to suppress the groan I'm feeling.

Please let it be a stranger. Please let it be someone random looking for directions, or thinking I'm their Uber ride.

It isn't.

Because of course it had to be.

Clay.

My best friend Annie's big brother.

An alpha – unlike his sister and their parents – all betas.

If I thought I had a thing about wonky wheels on trolleys and bad luck, I have an even bigger thing when it comes to Clay and embarrassing situations. He's just seen me with my tongue sticking out trying to catch snowflakes. This is not the most embarrassing interaction we've ever had. The first time I met him was when Annie and I were sharing a dorm room in the first year of college. He arrived when I had the world's worst cold. Think swollen nose, streaming eyes, and snot. Snot everywhere. I opened the door to him, thinking it was one of the other girls that lived on our hallway, dressed in my ancient hoodie and sweats, hair scraped back that hadn't been washed for, I confess, probably four days, and instead found not only a man standing the other side of the door, a hot man, a hot alpha. I proceeded to sneeze all over him. Yep. Great big globs of snot flying right at him.

The second time I met him, I was so embarrassed about the first time that I fumbled my desk drawer and sent my bright neon pink vibrator buzzing across the dorm room floor. And the final time we met, several years ago now, at our college graduation, I nearly took his eye out with my graduation cap.

On all three of these occasions, the alpha with the stick shoved up his backside had just stood in silence, staring me down with a withering look, making it clear how silly and pathetic he considered me to be.

Yep, me and Clay have history, but it's not the kind of history that alphas and omegas usually have. It's the kind of history that creeps up on you in the middle of the night, drowning you in embarrassment and reminding you just how cringingly awful your life is.

"Hey, Clay," I say.

We stand there, staring at each other.

Of course, he looks as gorgeous as he always has done. Tall. Broad. Solid. A jawline so sharp it could chisel marble. Lips unsuitable soft on such a manly-looking man. A full-head of richly dark hair and eyes clear blue like the morning sky.

He has one or two more lines drawn around those eyes than he did that first time we met, and he's even more well-built than he was back then, but he is definitely still hot. Hot Clay. Particularly today, dressed in a pair of faded jeans, an old padded jacket and a cowboy hat.

"Annie went inside looking for you," he says, pointing his thumb in the direction I've just come. "She was – "

He doesn't finish his sentence because he's interrupted by the biggest, most high-pitched squeal I've heard in a long time. And then my best friend, Annie, is sprinting toward me and flinging her arms around me, squeezing me as tightly as she can and even lifting me right off my feet. Annie is about a foot shorter than her ginormous brother, but she's still a good two or three inches taller than I am. She also has flaming red hair and the same blue eyes as her brother.

"Hollie!" she says, dropping me back down to my feet. "You're here! You're really actually here!"

"Of course I'm here!" I say, grinning so widely my cheeks might actually be splitting.

I can't help it when I'm around Annie. Her energy and enthusiasm are infectious, and it's impossible to be in a bad mood when you're with her. Well, it's impossible for me anyway. Her big brother Clay seems immune to his sister's high spirits; you couldn't get two people who are more polar opposites. Clay rarely smiles, rarely seems happy and rarely gets excited about anything. In fact, most of the time he looks unamused and unimpressed. Especially when small, snotty little omegas sneeze all over his face.

"I was beginning to panic," she says. "I was right by the exit gate watching for you. I even had a welcome sign and everything." She unravels a long sign, hand-drawn in an array of felt-tip colors.

I shrug. "I must have snuck right past." I hug her again, whispering in her ear, "You probably got distracted by that football team that was on my flight."

"Oh my goodness," Annie whispers back. "I've never seen so many hot men in one place."

"That," I say, "is because you live out in the middle of nowhere. If you were back in Rockview–"

"Yeah, yeah," she says, hooking her arm through mine and motioning her head toward the trolley with all the luggage.

Clay gets the hint and strides right toward it, pushing the thing with no effort at all. In fact, the misbehaving wheel now seems to have mended its bad behavior altogether. I'm not exactly surprised. There's something about Clay Jackson, something authoritarian, which means everybody does as he says and everybody behaves well in his presence. Well, at least most people do. Annie seems immune to her brother's superpowers just like he's immune to hers.

Clay and the trolley stride off determinedly in front of us, and Annie and I walk behind.

"How was your flight?" Annie said. "Did you manage to bag a seat next to any of those football players?"

"No," I say, "they were all in first class. I was stuck between an old lady with a fear of flying and a middle-aged man who thought I wanted to hear about his upcoming divorce."

"You poor thing. Probably in need of a stiff drink."

"Oh," I say, "I may have had one or two of those on the airplane."

"Good for you," Annie says as we walk onto the car lot, catching up with Clay, who's already loading my suitcases into the back of a smart-looking pickup truck.

"Is this yours?" I ask Annie.

She rolls her eyes. "Of course not. This is Clay's. My baby's at home."

"Her baby wouldn't make it out to the airport and back," Clay said. "It's unreliable. She needs to replace it."

"I most certainly do not," Annie says. "There's nothing unreliable about old Dina at all."

"Hmm," Clay says, opening the passenger door and letting Annie slide inside. I follow her in, and he shuts the door after us.

"Wow," I say.

"What?" Annie fastens her seatbelt and shifts round to look at me.

I lean in and whisper to her, "I don't think a man has opened a car door for me... ever."

Annie grins at me. "Welcome to Colorado, Hollie, where men – well, most men – have manners."

"Right," I say. "Maybe I am going to like it here."

"You're gonna love it," Annie says, taking my hand in hers and squeezing it. "And I'm so pleased you're here, Hollie. I couldn't bear the thought of you stuck all alone in your apartment back in Rockview. Not for the holidays."

Clay opens the driver's door next and jumps up into the seat in one swift move, slamming the door and revving the engine.

"She's going to really love it here, isn't she, Clay?"

Clay's eyes flick up to the rearview mirror, clear blue rimmed in a curtain of dark lashes. He meets my gaze with his usual indifference. "Depends," he says. "She might find it too cold."

"No, she won't," Annie says. "That's the best thing about this time of year. You can snuggle up by the fire, drink hot chocolate and watch the snow fall. Can't do any of that back in Rockview. Even in the middle of winter, it's still baking hot."

"Yeah," I say. "I quite like the idea of snuggling."

I'm probably mistaken or befuddled after the flight and the two glasses of wine, but I swear for just the briefest minuscule of seconds Clay Jackson's eyes seem to flash – that indifference vanishes for one swift moment. But then his attention is drawn to the front windshield as he pulls away from our parking spot and into the traffic.

"And you like snow too, right?" he says after another minute, his gaze flicking back up to the rearview mirror a second time. Am I imagining it again, or is there a slight tease in his eyes this time? "Like it enough to eat it."

Crap. He must have seen the whole tongue thing after all.

"I'm not sure," I say. "I think I'm going to love snow, but as my and snow's relationship has been short and brief, I can't make a judgement quite yet."

"What do you mean by short and brief?" Annie says.

"This is literally only the second time I've seen snow in my whole entire life," I say.

Annie squeals even louder than she did out by the front of the airport, jumping up and down on her seat. "Oh my goodness, Hollie. I had no idea."

"How can you be called Hollie," Clay says flatly, "and have only ever seen snow once before?"

"Because," I say, "my mom really, really loved Christmas."

The truck falls silent and Annie squeezes my hand again. Then she says, "Hollie, we're gonna take good care of you."

I smile back at her, trying not to let that flicker of sadness pull me into something more serious. Instead, I focus my attention on the window outside the truck. We're making our way through the city, and even out here where there's plenty of traffic and plenty of buildings, there's still a whole heap of snow everywhere I look. It makes everything look so pretty, so festive, so Christmassy.

And then we climb out of the city and up into the mountains and everything gets a whole heap more beautiful. It's as if I'm staring straight at a Christmas card scene. Fir trees dusted with snow, old wooden cabins all lit up with Christmas lights, snow blanketing the mountains and all the fields.

I always considered myself a city girl. I've lived in Rockview all my life, and I love the place. But this – this is enough to have the sadness lifting from my heart.

Yes, this was the right thing to do. Okay, it will be strange this year, not spending Christmas with my mom like I always have, not having our own little traditions, not having her, but being with Annie and her family – even if that does include her big, grumpy brother – is going to be a good thing. It's better than being home alone with just my goldfish, Ted, for company. That, I suspect, would have been a bad decision.

Although there's one problem with this carefully crafted master plan.

The big, grumpy alpha. He smells of home-baked brownies. The kind made with real dark chocolate, the kind that are soft and sticky in the middle, the kind that give you an almost orgasm as soon as you bite into them.

Yeah, I'd forgotten just how heavenly his scent is, which could make Christmas just that little bit more challenging.

Chapter Two

C lay

I thought I'd gotten over my feelings for Hollie Bright. I thought I'd gotten over her a long, long time ago. After all, it's been ten years since I first laid eyes on the little omega.

But as soon as I spot her spinning in the snow outside the airport, arms flung wide, head tipped back, pretty blue eyes sparkling with excitement, caramel hair caught in the wind, I realize I'm in trouble.

Big trouble.

I am most definitely not over Hollie Bright.

My crush on my little sister's college roommate – my little sister's now longest, oldest, and bestest friend – was fine when, all those years ago, our interactions were sparse and brief. But this time, the omega is spending a whole damn week with us. With my family. At our ranch. And it's not just any week; it's Christmas week.

Sure, I can keep myself busy on the ranch. There's always plenty to do. But there are still going to be family occasions where I won't have an excuse to disappear and when I am most definitely going to be in the omega's company.

I swallow hard, hands white-knuckling the steering wheel of my truck, and try my best not to suck in the sweet little thing's scent. If she weren't so darn cute, with a curvy little figure to die for, I'd say Hollie Bright's scent was the best thing about the omega. It smells like... like honey. The kind of honey you want to drizzle all over your bread in the morning. The kind of honey you want to drizzle all over your tongue. The kind of honey you want to sink your fingers into and lick them clean.

It was her scent that hit me first all those years ago. Hit me like a slap around the face. Like a bucket of cold water over the head. Like a punch to the gut. *Wake up, mother-fucker, and take notice; something special has entered your life.* Turned out Hollie Bright was more than just special. She was the type of girl you couldn't keep your eyes off when she entered a room, the kind of girl who had you entranced when she spoke, the only girl who's ever made my stupid heart actually flutter with one of her smiles.

And the kind of girl who has never been interested in alphas.

I shake my head and focus on the road ahead. The drive back home seems to last twice as long as the drive out to the airport, and I blame that entirely on Hollie Bright's honey scent and the way it has my taste buds tingling and my blood buzzing.

Finally – goddamn finally – we reach the outer boundary of the ranch, passing from the main road onto the track and bumping along, passing under the big sign that marks our land: Big Sky Ranch.

"This is it?" Hollie asks. "This is the ranch?"

"Yep," Annie says, with a definite hint of pride in her voice.

"Wow," Hollie gasps.

And am I crazy, but I can't help a sense of pride myself at her obvious admiration. Then again, who wouldn't admire Big Sky Ranch? Of course I'm biased, but I happen to think it's the most beautiful ranch in the whole of Colorado – scrap that – probably in the whole of the country.

We pass by one of our winter pastures where part of the Hereford herd is huddled together, and Annie points them out.

"Aren't they cold?" Hollie asks almost immediately.

"No," I tell her. "Cattle are hardy. They're built for weather like this."

"Really?" she says. "But what do they eat?"

"Hay!" Annie says, giggling. She leans forward in her seat. "Hollie is a big animal lover." I don't need reminding. I happen to have catalogued and stored away every bit of information my sister has ever mentioned in passing about her best friend. "Clay, expect to answer a whole host of animal welfare questions while she's here."

I snort. "You're one of those... vegans, are you?"

"No," Hollie says. I sigh in relief. "I'm a vegetarian."

"I can't help thinking that's worse," I mutter.

"Don't listen to him," Annie says. "My dad is actually super excited about the prospect of cooking for a vegetarian this Christmas. He has about a million different recipe ideas he wants to run past you."

"I'm happy with just a block of cheese or a boiled egg," Hollie says.

And I snort again. Omegas may be tiny, but everyone knows they need to eat well. There can't be a lot of protein and nutrients in a lump of cheese.

We drive past the second pasture. Tucker's out on this one on the back of Storm, breaking ice on the water trough. He spots us too, knocking the hat off his head and swinging it in circles above his head, waving at all of us. Annie waves back.

"That's Tucker," she says.

"Ah," Hollie says. "Who's Tucker?"

I fidget in my seat.

"Oh," Annie says, innocently – although I wonder if my little sister Annie is ever innocent. She's been wrapping the lot of us around her little finger ever since she was born 29 years ago. "Tucker is one of Clay's ... pack mates."

There's silence in the car – a loaded one – and it takes all my self-control not to peer into the rearview mirror at Hollie's face.

I do not care about her reaction.

I do not care. I repeat, I do not care.

"P-p-pack," she mumbles at last, the unease in her voice automatically setting off a reciprocating unease in my body.

Obviously, I do care.

"Oh yeah, didn't I tell you?" Annie says, still sounding suspiciously innocent, as if this was a casual piece of information that just so happened to slip her mind. "Yeah, Clay's pack mate. Tucker."

"You have a pack?" Hollie says, this time directing her question to me. "Since when did you have a pack?"

"Since a year and a half ago," I say. This time I can't help but peer at her reflection. She looks shocked. Utterly shocked. And I wonder why it's so hard to believe that a man, an alpha like me, could be part of a pack. Okay, I know I can be an asshole. Stubborn. Seclusive. Downright irritating sometimes. But that doesn't mean I don't get along with people. And it doesn't mean that I didn't want to form a pack.

And I'm in a good position to form a pack now. I'm running the family ranch, and luckily I've found two alphas who love the work, who love the ranch, just as much as I do. We bonded over cattle driving. It was always inevitable that when I stepped up to take over the family business, they'd want to do it with me and we'd make it official. We'd become a pack.

Plus, every sensible alpha – every alpha in his right mind – wants a pack. And a little omega to go with that pack.

"There's me, Tucker, and Nash," I say. "Just the three of us."

"Just three," Annie chuckles.

But I don't see what's so funny about that.

"And they're basically running the ranch now," Annie says. "Dad's knee's gotten so bad he can't really do much around the ranch anymore. They've basically taken it over."

"Yeah," I say.

"And they're doing a pretty good job."

"Gee, thanks," I say.

"You're welcome," Annie says, blowing me a kiss.

We continue down the bumpy track, the girls bouncing in the back seat, Hollie much quieter than she has been for the rest of the drive. I wonder whether she regrets coming. I know a pack isn't every omega's dream. In fact, some omegas steer clear of packs altogether, packs and alphas. Hollie has always been one of those omegas; from the little snippets of information I've gleaned over the years, it's clear she's only ever dated betas. Which is fine. Just dandy. A-okay. Because I don't need to be mixing myself up with Hollie Bright.

I was there when Annie asked my parents if Hollie could visit over Christmas. I know how worried my little sister has been about her oldest friend, how anxious she is to ensure this festive period is perfect for her. I'm more than aware of what the woman needs right now and it isn't me.

Besides, Hollie Bright is a city girl. Always has been, always will be, and I don't need the distraction of a fling with a girl I've been thinking about for the last ten years. It would only lead to a lot more thinking in the long run.

Finally, as we swing past a small copse of trees, the old family home comes into view, its many windows a soft pink in the winter's sunlight and the wooden porch that runs the entirety of the house decorated with fir branches, sprigs of holly and bunches of mistletoe.

"This is it!" Annie cries, pointing out of the front wind-shield. "This is the old family house, built by my great-great-great-grandfather in 1874."

"It's that old?" Hollie says.

"You better believe it," Annie says. "Which is why every floorboard creaks and every tap leaks."

"Virtually the only original thing remaining are the foundations," I add. "Obviously it's had a lot of updating and renovation since 1874."

"Yeah," Annie says with a grin, "there's heating and everything. Even running water and flushing lavatories."

"Lavatories. Good to know," Hollie says. "I'm not sure I fancy the idea of trekking through the snow to some outback toilet."

I pull up outside the house, and I'm guessing my

parents must hear the truck 'cause they come out to greet us, my mom practically sprinting down the front steps. She has almost as much energy as my little sister.

"Hollie, sweetheart," she says, enveloping the smaller omega in one of her renowned hugs, locks of silvery red hair slipping loose from her bun. "I was so sorry to hear about your mom, and I'm so glad you're here," she says.

I don't know if Hollie is a hugger or not, but she has no choice but to stand and take the hug my mom's offering. And then my dad's there too. He's definitely not a hugger, but he pats her on the shoulder.

"How you doing, kid?" he asks her.

"Good," Hollie says. "I'm good – thank you – and very grateful to you both for letting me come stay."

"Nonsense," my mom says. "The more, the merrier."

"And it's going to be particularly merry this year," my dad says. "Clay's pack, Annie home and you too, Hollie. I don't think we've ever had this many people for Christmas."

"Think you can cope?" Annie asks my dad, nudging him lightheartedly with her elbow.

He places his hands on his hips and puffs out his chest. "I think I can rise to the challenge."

Since my dad's knee gave way 18 months ago and stopped him from taking a more active role in the running of the ranch, he's discovered a passion for cooking. Some might call it an obsession. I blame that damn show, The Great British Bake-Off. For the first two weeks after he did his knee, all he could do was sit and watch TV with his leg stretched out in front of him. He watched a hell of a lot of that show. Since then he's been creating all sorts in the kitchen and I'm having to work extra hard on the ranch to keep off the pounds.

"Well, come on," my mom says. "Let's not stand around

out here in the cold. Let's take you inside and warm you up. Clay, you can bring the bags, right?"

I tip my hat at my mom to signal my consent and watch as my mom and sister lead the little omega up the steps, across the porch, and through the door, disappearing inside.

I guess I must stand and watch a little too long because my dad hobbles alongside me, leans in, and says, "I forgot how pretty she was."

"Huh?" I say, shaking my head.

"Pretty. Hollie's really quite something to look at."

"I hadn't noticed."

My dad's silver eyes, always piercing, assess me. He doesn't say anything else, simply nods and waits for me to collect the suitcases. In the old days, there's no way my dad wouldn't have taken one himself. He's always prided himself on his strength and his can-do attitude – got a burst pipe, he'll mend it, burst tyre, he'll replace it, 100 head of cattle that need wrangling, he's on it. But now, with the knee, he's resigned to the sidelines in more than one way. I'm secretly glad about it. I think, given half the chance, my dad would have worked himself right the way into his own grave – heck, he'd probably have dug that grave too, save everyone else the job. He's worked hard all his life, very hard, and it's about time he put his feet up and had some fun. Even if that fun wasn't exactly what I was expecting. Still, at least it's not knitting.

I carry the bags through into the house, definitely not noticing how Hollie's honey scent has already infused into our home and definitely not thinking about just how pretty the little omega is.

Chapter Three

H ollie

As we stroll through the front door, a black and white border collie comes zooming across the floorboards toward us, tail wagging so quickly from side to side it's one continuous blur. The dog barks happily at me and jumps around my feet.

"Who – who is this?" I say, dropping down to crouch almost immediately and opening up my arms wide. The dog comes racing toward me, sniffing at me at first before dragging its tongue up my face.

"Dolly!" Mr. J snaps, clicking his fingers. "Manners."

Dolly responds almost immediately, jumping back and dropping to lie down, although her tail continues to sweep across the floor in excitement.

"Dolly," Annie says. She bends down to pat the dog on the head. "She used to be Dad's working dog, but she's retired now too. And if Dolly's here, that means somewhere around here is – ah, yeah, there – Kenny."

I follow the direction in which my best friend is pointing and, to my surprise, see a large, snowy white rabbit lingering in the corner, little nose twitching up and down.

"A rabbit?" I say.

"Yes," Annie says. "He's a house rabbit."

"He was meant to be an outdoor rabbit," Mrs. J says. "But someone is a big softie." I'm assuming she means Annie. "And couldn't stand the idea of him being outside in the cold."

"Don't dogs eat rabbits?" I say, watching in astonishment as the old collie strolls back to the bunny and flops down beside him, the bunny immediately curling up with the dog.

"Greyhounds, maybe," Annie says. "But not Dolly. Dolly loves Kenny nearly as much as Kenny loves Dolly. They're inseparable. In fact, I think Kenny might think that he's actually a dog. Watch this. Kenny! Kenny!" Annie calls. "Come!"

Kenny looks up from where he seems extremely comfortable. One of his ears twitches.

"Kenny, come!" Annie says more firmly this time.

Reluctantly, the bunny slumps up and then hops over to my best friend. My best friend tickles between his ears and I give her a little applaud.

"I've never known a rabbit who could follow commands before."

"He doesn't always do it," Annie confesses. "I think he's just showing off for your benefit."

"Right," Mrs. J says. "Let's warm you up, Hollie."

And next she's leading me through into a giant family kitchen, which is probably the size of my Rockview apartment. She forces me down onto a stool, and then she's pouring us out hot chocolates she's been cooking on the stove. It's creamy, warm, and utterly delicious. And it does not make me think of the alpha who I spy from the corner of my eye carrying both of my suitcases up the staircase.

After the hot chocolate and one of Mr. Jackson's home-baked chocolate chip cookies, Annie takes me on a tour of the house. It really is beautiful, like something right out of Little House on the Prairie. The views from each window are picture perfect and everything is knotted wooden floorboards made cozy with homemade quilts and thick rugs.

When we've toured nearly all the rooms, I ask as innocently as I can, "So where's Clay's room?"

"I showed you," Annie says, pointing ahead of us. "That one back there."

"But," I say, "how about his pack mates?"

Annie gives me a guilty little smile. "Are you angry with me, Hollie?" she asks.

"Angry?" I say. "Why would I be angry?"

"For not telling you about the pack thing. Your mom got sick about the same time Clay got together with his pack. So, I guess I never really told you about it at the time. And then, I don't know, I just forgot. I forgot it was a big deal for an omega."

"Oh," I say, really wishing and willing my cheeks not to pinken. "It's not a big deal. It's fine. I was just curious because there don't seem to be enough bedrooms, and there's only one bed in Clay's room and it's a single bed at that." Something I find surprising for an alpha – an alpha that smells the way he does and looks as hot as he does.

Unless, when he's hooking up with the countless women that he must be hooking up with, he always goes back to their place.

"That's his old bedroom, his childhood bedroom." Which makes a lot of sense now I come to think about it, given the model racing cars, the dinosaur bedsheets, and all the comics. "Clay and his packmates are staying in one of the cabins out on the ranch until they've built their own house."

"They're building their own house? Where?"

"On the ranch, silly," Annie says.

"On the ranch?" I cry. "Geez, how big is this place?"

"10,000 acres, Hollie. Plenty of room. They wanted to build their own house for their own family."

"Oh," I say again, this time concentrating with all my might on not letting my cheeks burst into flame. Of course – *of course* – Clay Jackson would have a pack – a pack that includes that seriously hot cowboy I saw out there on his horse in the field. Of course, Clay Jackson and his hot packmate would have an omega. Of course, Clay Jackson, his hot packmate and their omega would be on the verge of starting a family. Of course, some girl would already have snapped them up. That's just logical.

"So... they're starting a family?"

"Well, not yet," Annie says. "They've got to build the house first."

"Right," I say. "And are they going to get married?"

My best friend looks at me like I've lost my mind. "You know Clay isn't gay, right? I mean, I know I don't talk a lot about my big brother, but I think I've mentioned girlfriends in the past."

"I wasn't suggesting he was gay."

"You just asked me if he was married. I assume you meant to his packmates."

"No, no, I meant – " I can feel myself digging a hole, and I wish, in some ways, I was, then I could fall right into it and the earth could swallow me up. Or maybe now would be the perfect time for aliens to swoop down and abduct me. I wish I'd never started this conversation. "You said they were starting a family. I assume they're starting a family with, you know, a girl."

"Ahhhh," Annie says, with a hint of a smile. "You're asking me if they're dating anyone."

"I was not asking you whether they were dating anyone."

"You so were," she says.

"Well, are they?" I ask, crossing my arms over my chest.

"Hollie Bright," Annie says, also crossing her arms over her chest and mirroring my prickly posture. "Are you interested in my brother? Because that is kind of gross."

"Is it?" I ask.

"Totally," she says. "My best friend and my brother." She makes a gagging face.

"I'm not interested," I tell her. Okay, possibly I am a little bit interested. I bet there isn't an omega on the planet who wouldn't be interested in Clay Jackson – despite his obvious downsides – that grumpy attitude being the most obvious one. There are enough upsides – the good looks, the countless endless number of muscles and that mouthwatering scent.

But in my experience, alphas are problems. They may look hot, they may smell delicious, they may do things to an omega's body that an omega just can't control, but they're also arrogant, uptight, and rude. And Clay Jackson, in my experience, is all three of those things. I'm definitely not interested in him and his scrummy scent or his obscenely big biceps or his tight-fitting jeans. Not at all.

"I'm glad we got that cleared up then," Annie says, narrowing her eyes at me. "Shall we continue the tour now?"

"Yes," I say.

"You sure?" she asks. "You don't want to go sniff my brother's bedsheets?"

"Annie!" I yelp.

"Sorry, Hollie. I just thought that was the kind of thing you omegas did."

Annie grew up with an elder brother who (according to her) presented as an alpha in his early teens. She lived with me – an omega – all the way through college and grad school. Yet, she continues to play ignorant when it comes to alpha and omega dynamics.

"Annie," I say, "you've known me ten whole years. Since when have I gone round sniffing men's sheets?"

"There's always a first time for everything," she says. I stick my tongue out at her. She sticks hers right back out at me. "Want to go and see the animals now?"

Which is most definitely her attempt at a peace offering, because Annie knows I love animals. I've been obsessed with them ever since I was a little girl. It's the reason I'm vegetarian. It's the reason I spent nearly all of my twenties training to be a vet. Unfortunately, I grew up with a mom who was highly allergic to every animal on the planet. So I never had any pets at home other than the one stick insect that died after two weeks. I guess I could have got a pet once I'd moved out, but there aren't a lot of landlords in Rockview who are particularly happy accepting an omega in the first place. I guess they don't like the idea of our scents sinking into the walls or our slick ruining the furnishings. There definitely aren't many landlords willing to accept an omega with pets in toe as well. That's why I have Ted, the goldfish, and rely on the clinic for my daily-dose of animal snuggles.

"You mean the horses?" I ask Annie.

"I mean the horses," she replies.

Out of all the animals in the universe, I love horses the most. It all started with a *My Little Pony* craze when I was in kindergarten, then morphed to an obsession with *The Pony Club* books as a tweenie, and it hasn't really stopped since then. I love horses, even if I rarely get the chance to ride them.

"Come on then," Annie says, taking my hand and pulling me down the stairs and back out into the snow. It really is brutally cold out here in Colorado. It hits you like a wall of ice, like stepping into a freezer. I tug up the collar of my jacket and follow Annie across the yard toward the big barn. I instantly realize that sneakers were a poor choice for vacation footwear, because, almost immediately, the cold snow is sinking into the leather and my feet are already wet. However, nothing – not even frozen toes and losing limbs to frostbite – is going to distract me from what's about to happen.

Annie leads me inside the barn, and I think I am in horse heaven.

"Oh my goodness," I say. "They're all so beautiful." There are six horses, each occupying a stall of their own. Three are a dark chestnut color, their coats shiny. Two are mottled white, brown, and black. And the final could easily be Black Beauty himself – he's the color of night, and his coat is so sleek I think I could almost see my face reflected back in it.

"Let me introduce you to them," Annie says. "This is

Bonnie," she says, pointing to the first chestnut. "And this is Clyde," she says, pointing to the next. "And then this is Sugar, because she has the sweetest nature of any horse you could meet."

I say hi to each of the three horses, giving them an obligatory little scratch on the nose.

"Then this is Cloud," she says, pointing to the more white of the horses. "And this – this is Dust," she says, pointing to the other.

I stroke them both too.

"And then finally, last but not least, is Jet."

I think I fall in love with Jet almost immediately. Not only is he, frankly, the most beautiful horse I've ever seen in my life, he also nudges his nose against my hand and demands my attention.

"So," I say, "who belongs to who?"

"Sugar is mine," Annie says. "Bonnie and Clyde are Mom and Dad's."

"And let me guess," I say, "Jet belongs to Clay?" That man was designed to ride a black horse.

"Yeah," she says. "Correct."

I spend the next ten minutes reveling in horse heaven, feeding each of the horses some treats and stroking and petting them. By now my feet are well and truly solid blocks of ice, and we're just about to leave and make our way back to the house when the barn door swings open and who I think must be the cowboy we saw out in the field earlier walks through leading a gray horse. Except it's not the cowboy from earlier. It's a different one. The cowboy out in the field looked like something straight out of a John Wayne movie – Levi jeans, spurs on his boots and a wide-brimmed hat. This cowboy wears a pair of glasses – all steamed up as he steps through into the warmth of the barn, a button down jacket and cord pants. A mop of thick hay-colored hair flops into his chestnut eyes as he slides off his glasses and wipes the lenses on his sleeves.

"Hey, Nash," Annie says.

The man stops in his tracks and blinks at the two of us. "Uh, hi," he says, managing a shy smile.

"This is my best friend, Hollie."

He nods, sliding his glasses back into place, and looping the reins of the horse around the nearest post. He strides toward me and holds out his hand. His scent hits me almost immediately. He smells of bookshops. It's so surprising I almost gasp. I've always loved the smell of books, especially a new one – it's the second best present someone could gift me after a bunny, a dog or a cat – and I can't help but wonder what it can mean.

"Nash," he says, holding out his hand. "Nice to meet you, Hollie."

I shake his hand. It's large, his grip strong and his fingers calloused.

"This is Clay's other packmate," Annie explains.

"Hi," I manage to squeak back at the man who's examining me through his glasses.

"Good to have you here, Hollie," he says.

He's still holding my hand, and if I'm honest, I'm not really sure I want him to let it go, but I remember I'm not here to ogle at alphas. I'm here to mend my broken heart and try to forget why this Christmas could possibly be the saddest of my life.

I motion at the horse he's just led into the barn. "Who's this?" I ask him.

"Ah," he says, strolling back toward the horse and beckoning me to follow him. He strokes his hand affectionately down the horse's long, gray neck. "This is Jane," he says.

"Jane," I repeat. "That's an unusual name for a horse."

"It's after my favorite author," he says.

I frown. I don't recall the name of any famous thriller or crime writers called Jane.

"Jane Austen," he says.

I try not to let my jaw hit the floor. An alpha – an alpha who likes Jane Austen, who likes Jane Austen so much he's named his horse after her.

"Is that a joke?" I ask.

"Why would that be a joke?" he asks me, frowning right back at me.

"Er, nothing," I say. "She's a beauty."

"Yeah, best horse a man could have," he says, patting her neck. "She's worked hard today. Time for a rest." He unhooks the reins and leads her to one of the empty stalls.

"Hollie's absolutely nuts about horses," my best friend tells the alpha.

I go to open my mouth to argue, but Nash beats me to it. "Then we'll have to take you out riding with us. Show you a bit of the countryside. In my opinion, it's the most beautiful there is."

"But you're not from here originally," I say. His voice has a more southern twang.

"Yeah," he says. "I grew up down South." He looks me up and down. "You should ride Cloud. I think she'd suit you."

"Oh," I say. "I haven't ridden in ages."

The man blinks at me twice and frowns again. "You love horses, but you don't ride."

"Yeah," I say. "I guess I've been pretty busy." With work

and caring for my mom. The unsaid words hang heavy in the air.

"Well," he says, "we'll have to change that, won't we?"

And before I can argue a second time, he disappears inside the stall.

"That's a great idea," Annie says, grabbing my cold hand in hers. "We'll do loads of riding while you're out here – that's if the weather allows."

"So," I say as we step back outside into the snow-covered landscape, the now setting sun christening every-thing a rosy pink color that has my heart warming even more than it already was, "what's the plan tonight? Are we going to open a bottle of wine and catch up? Or watch a Christmas movie? Or if you need help wrapping any presents I can ..."

"No flipping way," my best friend says, pinching my arm. "This is your first night in Silver Creek. There's only one thing we're doing tonight."

"There is," I say. "What's that?"

"We're getting dressed up and we're going dancing."

Chapter Four

Nash

Tucker arrives on Storm ten minutes after Annie and her friend leave the barn. I've already finished with Jane, and I go and give him a hand, putting his horse to bed and checking up on the rest before we lock up the barn for the evening.

"You met Annie's friend yet?" I ask him as we bolt the door.

"Nope. Saw her briefly in the truck as Clay was driving past."

"Yeah," I say, scratching the side of my cheek. "Funny thing."

"Funny thing?" Tucker says.

"Yeah," I say. "Funny thing. Clay never mentioned how pretty she was."

Tucker lifts an eyebrow in my direction. He happens to

think I fall in love far too easily. He says I'm walking around willing my heart to be broken at every opportunity. He says I read too much romance. He probably doesn't believe me about the omega.

"Seriously," I say. "Seriously pretty."

"And she's an omega," Tucker says.

"We knew that already," I tell him.

"A pretty omega," Tucker says, one side of his mouth lifting in a smile. "Sounds like the perfect gift for Christmas to me."

"She's Annie's best friend," I remind him. "Off limits."

"Says who?"

"It's code. Family code," I tell him.

"Fuck, Nash," he says. "A hundred years ago you could marry a cousin. I don't think there's any problem with rolling around in the hay with your sister's best friend, especially if she's looking for some fun."

"The girl just lost her mom."

"So she needs cheering up," he says, that half-smile growing.

"Tucker," I warn him.

"Lighten up, Nash," he responds, plunging his hands inside his pockets as we stroll up to the big house.

"Why'd you think Clay never told us?" I ask my friend.

"That she was pretty? Maybe he doesn't find her pretty, Nash." I snort. He'd have to be blind not to find that girl pretty. "Or maybe she's just not his type."

"Yeah," I say, nodding my head. That's more likely. If I'm considered the packmate who falls in love too easily, then Clay is the exact opposite. He hardly ever falls. No one ever seems to meet up to his high expectations and towering standards.

We head into the kitchen. Mrs. J has left some tall

glasses of water out for us along with Mr. J's latest baking outputs. I pick up two of the cookies and down the water. Tucker does the same, peering his head round the kitchen door, clearly on the lookout for the Christmas visitor. He doesn't spot her, though he comes back into the kitchen, sniffing at the air.

"Oh man, do you smell that?"

I nod. Her scent suits her. It's hard to describe why, but I reckon if I'd smelled her first and closed my eyes and imagined a picture of her in my mind, I would have conjured up an image of the girl I met just now, out in the barn. Small, curvy, pretty, big blue eyes and rosy pink lips. I don't care what Tucker says – that I fall in love with everyone – Hollie is most definitely my type.

"Want to hang around?" Tucker says.

"No," I say. "I want to get cleaned up and then I want a drink."

Tucker nods, shoving a whole cookie into his mouth and then saying around it with his mouth full, "Sounds like a plan, my man."

It takes us fifteen minutes of walking through the snow to reach the cabin. We could have chosen to put the horses to bed in the barn by our cabin, but the one by the big house is warmer and more comfortable, and call us cold-hearted alphas, but we're big softies for those damn horses.

Clay's already In the cabin. It's glowing from the inside, and when we open the door we're met by the heat of the roaring fire he's started in the hearth.

"Hey," he says. He's sitting at the small kitchen table, his heels resting on the seat of another chair. "How were the fences?" he says. Now we're in the depths of December, the weather has turned for the worst and the cattle seem even more determined to break through any weaknesses in the fencing.

Tucker tells him and I describe the work I did mending the fences out on the lower northern pastures.

"How was your day?" Tucker says, dropping down into a chair and leaning forward, forearms resting on his knees, a big grin on his face.

"Just fine," Clay says, not quite meeting our packmate's eyes.

"Had fun at the airport?"

Clay shrugs.

Tucker examines him for a moment, then leans right back on his chair and rests his hands in his lap. "Nash thinks she's pretty."

"Nash thinks every woman on the planet is pretty."

"I do not," I protest. "But I do happen to think Hollie is pretty."

"What do you think, Clay?" Tucker asks.

"I think that's a judgement you should make for yourself, Tucker," he says.

"I haven't met her yet," Tucker bounces his leg on the spot, "but I'm definitely interested to meet her after catching her scent in the house. Man," he groans, "that – that omega smells like –"

"Be more respectful," Clay snaps.

Tucker erupts into a peal of laughter.

"I'm serious," Clay says. "She's my sister's best friend."

"That's what I said," I tell him. "She's not some toy you can mess around with."

Tucker groans like he's just been told by the teacher that, indeed, he can't play with the toy he's been eyeing and had better put it the hell away. "How many omegas are there in Silver Creek?" he asks us.

"Three," I answer.

"Exactly, three," Tucker repeats. "And how many of those are actually single?"

"Zero," I state.

"Zero," he repeats again. "Zero available omegas."

"There are hundreds, thousands of omegas in Colorado," Clay tells him. "Plenty for you to fuck around with."

"Yeah, but I'm working – working hard, Clay. Damn hard." Which is true. Tucker may be a bit of a joker, a bit of a ladies' man. He may have a reputation as a playboy, but he's one of the hardest working men I know. It's why the three of us get on so well. It's why we bonded. It's why we work so well as a pack. We're all dedicated to the job, to the work. We all want to see this ranch last for another one hundred and fifty years. We want our children to inherit it from us, and then our grandchildren, and their children, and their children after that.

"Where do I get the chance to meet omegas?" Tucker continues. "And now there's one here, landed right in our laps–"

"She's not landing in anyone's laps," Clay snaps.

"Figure of speech," Tucker says with one of his charming smiles. The kind of smile that has a lot of ladies dropping their panties.

"Fuck around with Hollie Bright," Clay tells Tucker, "and I will beat your ass."

"And what if she wants to fuck around with me?" he says.

"Unlikely," Clay tells him. "Hollie Bright's not interested in alphas."

"She's an omega," I state. "Of course she's interested in alphas."

Clay shakes his head. "She's not. She dates betas."

Tucker says nothing – for a moment he's speechless, which for our talkative, chatty friend is almost unheard of. "An omega who doesn't like alphas," he says, whistling. "That is strange."

"Yeah," Clay says. "Well, the girl is strange. The first time I met her, she sneezed right in my face. And the second time, she literally threw a vibrator at me."

"Are you sure she wasn't trying to flirt?" Tucker asks. "You're really bad at knowing when women are trying to flirt with you, Clay."

"I am not," he says.

"Oh, come on, man," Tucker teases. "You are – remember that girl at the bar, the one who stroked your arm and asked you questions about breeding Herefords?"

"I remember," I say. "Clay thought she was genuinely interested in starting her own farm."

Tucker laughs again. "Talking of bars," he says. "Are we going tonight?"

Clay kicks his feet off the chair and nods his head. "Yeah," he says. "I could do with a drink."

Chapter Five

H ollie

Considering we're most likely going to a dive bar tonight, I seem to be taking a lot more care than usual over my makeup and styling my hair. I try not to think too closely about the motives for this. Definitely not Clay Jackson and his two two hot pack mates – three alphas who don't even live in this house, who I am very unlikely to be bumping into tonight. Still, on the off chance, I want to look my best. And besides, Annie gave me strict instructions: No slouchy jeans, no oversized hoodies. Tonight is all about dressing up and having fun.

So I pull on a glitzy top, a short skirt and my stockings and head downstairs to meet my best friend. I find her back in the family kitchen with her mom and dad. And I'm relieved to find that she hasn't set me up. She's also dressed up tonight. In fact, she's wearing one of her legendary little black dresses.

"Wow," Mr. J says, whistling. "Don't you two look the part?"

Annie inspects me closely, signaling with her hand for me to spin. I oblige her and then she nods with satisfaction. "You look great, Hollie," she says. "You're going to have every cowboy in that bar drooling all over you."

"Hmm," I say, walking toward them all. "I'm not sure that's exactly what I want. That sounds a little bit gross."

Mr. J laughs and slides a bowl of pasta in my direction. There's another already waiting in front of Annie. "Eat up, girls," he says. "I know you haven't seen each other for a while. I know there's going to be drinks involved and I don't want anyone vomiting in my truck."

I glance at Annie. "Dad's offered to drive us to the bar and back. Our own personal Uber driver."

"Really?" I say. "Mr. J, that's really kind. You don't–"

"Don't be silly. I'm perfectly happy to do it. But, like I said, eat up."

He points at the creamy pasta. It smells divine and I don't have any problem following his instructions.

"What are we wearing on your feet, Hollie?" Mrs. J asks as I wolf down the dish.

"Oh," I say, swinging out my leg and peering down at my feet. "I guess my sneakers again?"

Annie drops her fork into her bowl, the action making a large clattering sound. "Hollie Bright," she says, "did you bring no suitable footwear?"

"What do you mean?" I ask.

She points toward the window, where it's snowing again. "There's a foot of snow out there. You can't wear sneakers. Did you bring no boots?"

I shrug. "I don't own any boots," I tell her. "I live in Rockview."

"What size are your feet, honey?" Mrs. J says, as everyone now glances at my feet and I really wish I didn't have a hole in my stockings and that my big toe wasn't poking right out of that hole like an ugly toadstool.

"I'm a size eight," I say.

"Perfect!" Mrs. J gasps, clapping her hands together and then darting from the room.

Annie shrugs, clearly as confused as I am by her mom's actions. A few minutes later, Mrs. J reappears, a pair of brown cowboy boots dangling form her hands as well as a pair of woolly socks.

"Here," she says, dropping them by my feet. "Try those on."

"Are you sure?" I say, examining the boots. They're clearly well made with a pretty white floral design up the sides. They look expensive and I'm known for my poor coordination. In my lifetime, I've condemned three pairs of expensive shoes to the garbage because of spilled drinks – and two weren't even mine. "I don't want to ruin them."

"Absolutely," she says. "Boots were made for wearing. And these are my lucky boots."

She glances toward Mr. J who winks back at her.

"Lucky. What does that mean?" my best friend says with suspicion.

"I was wearing these boots the night I met your dad," Mrs. J says, smiling at her husband.

"And she looked drop-dead gorgeous in them too."

"Ew," Annie says, "please don't say you were wearing these boots when Clay was conceived."

Mrs. J glares at her daughter. "Your brother was born

two years after we were married, and you know that perfectly well, young lady."

"I know," Annie says, "just teasing."

"These boots sound really special," I say to Mrs. J. "I couldn't wear them."

"'Course you can," she says. "It's good to spread the luck around. Besides, I haven't had a chance to wear them in ages. What with Paul's hurt knee, we can't go dancing anymore."

"I'll still take you dancing," Mr. J says, holding out his hand and pulling his wife toward him, spinning her around under his arm. She giggles and I realize just how in love Annie's parents still are.

"Wear the boots," Annie says. "Mom's right. We could do with some luck." She leans close to me and whispers right in my ear. "And you could do with getting laid? How long has it been?"

"Too long," I mutter.

"Exactly!"

"But *you* should wear them," I protest. "they're your parents–"

"They're two sizes too small for me," Annie yelps.

"And you need the luck too!"

Annie grins. "Nope." I gape at her. "I'll tell you about it later," she promises, "Now come on, put them on."

I pull on the woolen socks and then drop my feet into the left boot and then the right. I'm surprised to find, when I stand on my feet, that they're incredibly comfortable. And not only that, they look really cute.

"Are you sure?" I ask Mrs. J one last time.

"Wouldn't have offered them if I wasn't," she says. "Right, come on, Paul, get these girls out to the bar. They look too drop-dead gorgeous to be standing around in my kitchen."

The snow looks even prettier as we drive out to the bar, all lit up by the headlights of Mr. J's truck and reflecting the holiday lights of the few sparse properties we pass by along the way. After 15 minutes of bumpy track, we're back on the main road, and then another five and we hit Silver Creek, the nearest town. The bar, the *Dirty Boot*, sits on the far side which means I get a good chance to ogle this little mountain town as we drive through. There's a grocery and a hardware store, a diner and what looks like a bakery with a giant gingerbread house in its window. We also pass a few houses, and they look a million times more wintery and Christmassy than the houses back in Rockview with snow on their roofs, garlands hanging on their front doors and lights wound round the porches and the trees. I feel as if I've stepped right inside a Christmas movie.

Another a few more minutes, we've reached the other side of town and Mr. J is pulling up his truck outside what looks like a ramshackle old barn, the beat of music, laughter and voices already carrying across toward us on the cold air.

"This is it?" I say, leaning forward to peer out the window. "You got me all dressed up to come here!"

"Do not judge a book by its cover, Hollie Bright," Annie declares, swinging open the cab door and jumping down.

She beckons me to follow and I do, thanking Mr. J once more for the ride.

"I'll be here at 12 to pick you girls up – your own personal pumpkin – unless I hear otherwise."

Annie threads her arm through mine and leads me to the bar, the music booming even more loudly with every step closer we take.

I hiss at her, "Is this another one of your pranks? Are we gonna walk inside and everyone else is in baggy jeans and hoodies after all?"

"Hollie," she says, "this is the only place there is to go out dancing unless you fancy driving through the night. Trust me, everyone is going to be dressed in their best glad rags. Anyway," she says, shrugging, "since when do you care what people think?"

"Hello," I say, "always. I've always cared what people think. You know that."

"Well, you shouldn't," Annie says, leaning on the door and holding it open for me.

Warmth and even more noise blasts straight into my face and I see the bar is packed, absolutely packed. They're three deep around the bar itself, every table is occupied and there's a dance floor too, already full, a band on a stage at the back, playing their hearts out.

"Okay," I say to Annie, "I take it back."

Because she's right, everyone's dressed up, most people in their cowboy boots that they've definitely been shining, nearly every girl dressed either in a skirt, a dress, or jeans so tight they look like they could rip with any sudden movements, Men in shirts, hair gleaming with styling product. The aroma is overpowering, especially to an omega like me – a thick cloud of perfume, aftershave, hairspray and beer. For a moment it has my head spinning.

Annie grips my arm that bit tighter and leads me through the crowds of people. Several I notice looking our way. Several sweeping their gazes up and down our bodies.

"Jeez," I lean forward and hiss in Annie's ear. "Are you sure this outfit's okay? I feel like everyone's looking at me."

"Because you're a newbie," she says. "Everyone knows

everyone around here, and anyone new stands out like a sore thumb."

"Great," I say, "terrific."

"Stop moaning," she says. "Let's get some tequila."

Annie's only a couple of inches taller than me, and is way more upbeat than her brother, yet she still seems to conduct his air of dominance. In fact, at times she can be downright scary. She has no problem pushing her way through the crowds hovering by the bar, several giant-looking cowboys stepping right out of her way and letting her pass through, until finally we reach the bar itself.

It takes Annie no time to be served and I gather that's because one of the barmen serving tonight has an almighty big crush on my best friend. In fact, his whole face lights up like the Christmas trees I've seen outside when he spies her, bypassing all the other clients waiting to come serve us first.

"Hollie," my friend shouts, because it's hell of a noisy in this place, "This is Travis. Travis, Hollie."

We shake hands over the bar and then Annie's telling him to line up four shots of tequila – two each.

Travis winks at Annie and then gets to work and I shout right back in her ear, "Got anything to tell me about this 'Dude'?"

Annie pinches me. "Let's just say my sex drought has well and truly ended."

I look the man over. He's wearing a denim shirt, the sleeves rolled up, his forearms strong and covered in inks. Dark stubble covers his chin and his eyes are dark too. Just my friend's type. I can see why she wanted to come here and why she wanted to dress up.

Travis lines up four shot glasses in front of us, drizzling the tequila along the row and, and then slamming a little pot of salt and two slices of lime down in front of us too.

"Thank you, Travis," Annie says with a flirtatious smile.

"My pleasure, sweetheart," he chimes right back, the two of them eye fucking each other.

I cough loudly, snapping Annie out of it before she's tempted to leap over the bar and climb the barman.

"Ready?" Annie ask. Pouring some of the salt onto her hand and then some onto mine.

I peer at the tequila. Me and Annie used to go out drinking a lot back in our college days. But since she left town, and my mom got sick, I've spent more time on my sofa in front of the TV than I have down at any bars. My tolerance for alcohol must definitely have taken a nosedive. Still, there's no way I'm backing out now, and I think with all the eyes of the townsfolk on me tonight, I'm going to need a bit of Dutch courage.

"Ready," I say, dragging my tongue along the salt. My friend does the same.

Then, I pick up my shot glass as Annie picks up hers. We tap them together and then Annie's counting down. "Three, two, one."

I tip my head back, throwing the drink into my mouth and swallowing it straight away. It's about a million times stronger than I'm expecting and immediately I'm coughing and spluttering, my eyes watering.

"Lime!" Annie shouts.

I pick it up and shove it in my mouth, sucking furiously. I can already feel the mascara I carefully applied onto my eyelashes swimming down my face.

Of course, it is at this moment precisely that the cowboy from the field – looking somehow hotter than he did several hours ago – pushes his way through the crowd and joins us.

"Hey," he says, tipping his hat in a way that makes my stomach flip.

I suck on the lime desperately, blinking furiously, tears streaming down my cheeks.
Crap.

Chapter Six

T ucker

"I think the lady needs some water," I tell Travis.

The Omega starts shaking her head desperately.

"Oh no, I'm fine," she chokes out, although she's sucking on that lime so violently, it's giving me ideas.

I nod my head to Travis and he fills a glass from the tap, handing it to me. I offer it to the omega. She spits out the lime into her hand and gulps the water furiously.

"Not a big drinker, I take it," I say.

"She used to be," Annie says from beside her friend.

"I guess I'm out of practice," the Omega says. She swipes her fingers under her eyes and blinks up at me. "You're the cowboy from the field."

"Yes, ma'am," I say, tipping my hat. "Tucker." I hold out my hand.

"Hollie," she says, sliding her hand into mine. It's small

and soft and warm, and I have a violent urge to pull the little thing right against my body, sweep her up into my arms, throw her in my truck, and drive her straight back to the cabin.

Nash wasn't lying. For once, he wasn't exaggerating. The little thing sure is cute. Cute and pretty. Shit, I'd even go as far as saying she's beautiful – all big blue eyes, long eyelashes, rosy cheeks, and plush lips just dying to be kissed.

"And what's a nice girl like you doing in a place like this?" I ask.

"Annie," she says. "She's always been a bad influence on me."

"Have not," Annie says. "It was you who once convinced me to sneak into that music festival without paying, and you who nearly got us arrested for public exposure on the beach when you decided we should sunbathe topless."

"I don't know what you're talking about," Hollie says, giggling.

I can't help smiling at the girl. Even her giggle is darn cute. I motion to the shot of tequila. "Is that yours too?"

She nods, and I pick it up in my hand.

"Hey," she says. "You're not stealing that, are you?"

"I wasn't planning on stealing it," I say. "I was planning on saving you from it. I'm not sure you can take another."

"I've only had one," she says.

"Plus the two glasses of wine on the airplane," Annie helpfully reminds her.

"That was hours ago," Hollie says, shaking her hand in my direction. "Sure, I can handle it."

"Okay," I say, "but don't say I didn't warn you."

I watch as she sprinkles salt on the back of her hand,

sliding her tongue along it – an action that's giving me another set of ideas. Then she tips that tequila down her throat, and with her eyes slammed shut, gropes around for her mauled piece of lime. I reach over the bar, find a fresh piece, and press it straight into her mouth. She opens her eyes, blinking up at me, because, well, my fingers are now in her mouth.

"Not bad," I say.

She sucks on the lime, taking it from my grip.

I shake my head at the two women in front of me. "I can't believe you brought her to the Dirty Boot on her first night in Silver Creek, Annie Jackson."

"And where else should I have taken her, Tucker Parker?"

"Anywhere but here," I say, as Hollie scans the busy bar.

"Actually, I think I like it here," she says. "It has a certain atmosphere."

"That's the tequila speaking," I tell her. But I motion my head toward the band. "Music's not bad, though."

"Yeah," she says. "I kind of like it."

"Kinda?" I ask.

"I'm more into pop, not really a country girl."

I shake my head. "Don't be saying that in a place like this, Hollie Bright – not if you want to walk out alive."

She laughs, although I'm pretty serious about that one.

"So, you've come to stay with us for a week, have you?"

"I've come to stay with *Annie*," she corrects.

"For ten days," Annie interjects.

"Ten days." Those words have never sounded so sweet – nearly as sweet as the Omega's scent itself.

"Well," I tell her, "you're very welcome here in Silver Creek."

"Thank you," she says.

I nod, catch Travis's attention, and a moment later I have an ice-cold beer in my hand. I take a swig. She's watching the band and the dancers, Annie now, as usual, engrossed in Travis MacCarthy.

I step closer to my packmate's sister's best friend. And honestly, what's Nash worried about? The degrees of separation couldn't be any further.

"I'm sorry about your mom," I say.

Her eyes flick my way, and for a moment I see a deep sadness hovering in her pretty eyes. Then her gaze flicks away, down to the floor. My gaze follows instinctively, and I see she's wearing a pair of cowboy boots. I'm not sure they've ever looked so good on a girl before.

"Thanks," she says. "It was... it was a while ago now."

"Still hurts though, doesn't it?" I say. "When you lose your mom."

She bites on her bottom lip and nods.

"It's good you came, Hollie," I say. "No one should be alone at Christmas, especially after that."

She nods again.

"You lost your mom too?" she asks.

"Yeah," I say. "Back when I was just a kid. Still miss her every day, though, especially at Christmas time."

"It's strange," she says. "I kind of want to forget about it. And I kind of... don't."

"Yeah," I say. "I understand."

Her eyes flick back up to mine again, and damn, Nash has never been so right. The girl really is pretty, especially with the neon lights from the bar falling across her smooth skin.

"Well," I tell her, "if you want to take your mind off things, I'm always happy to help."

Her eyes widen in shock, and I almost choke on my beer, realizing my misstep. I grin, laugh. "Geez, I didn't mean it that way. You have a dirty little mind, sweetheart."

She frowns at me. "You never can tell with Alphas."

Which is fair. I could easily, so easily, have meant it that way.

"I was just meaning there's a lot to do here in Silver Creek, especially down at the ranch. I hear you're keen on horses."

"I love them," she says, that frown melting away instantly. "I love all animals. I'm a vet."

"Are you now?" I say, because that ticks off about a billion other things I like in a woman – in an Omega. Clever, caring, good with animals. Honestly, why is Clay saying this girl is off-limits? Remind me, please.

"Yeah, well, we're going to take you out riding then," I tell her, "and then there's skating down on the lake and a ride up to the top of the mountain."

"Ah!" She nods enthusiastically.

"And also," I say, motioning my head toward the dance floor, "there's the good ole country pastime of line dancing. Want to try that now?"

She shakes her head. "Oh my goodness, no. I'm a horrible dancer, a really horrible dancer. I don't have two left feet, I have two malfunctioning limbs with the inability to coordinate them at all."

"Everyone can dance," I tell her. "And as far as I can tell, you have a perfectly good pair of legs."

My gaze drifts back down her legs, lingering on her ample thighs and tracking right down to those cowboy boots. She'd have a right to tell me off this time, because I definitely say it with a whole heap of flirtation.

"Not me," she says. "I can't dance. I never know what to

do, I always feel self-conscious. I usually end up falling on my ass."

"Yeah," I say, swigging the last of my beer and slamming it down on the bar. "But that's the good thing about line dancing. You just follow everyone else. There's no free will or interpretation in it. Honestly, you'll be just fine."

She grimaces and glances at her best friend, who's now completely engrossed in Travis, who seems to be taking a break from his bar duties altogether. She swings her gaze back to me.

I hold out my hand and give her my most charming smile. "Come on, you only live once," I tell her, "and I promise," I lean closer toward her, "I'll take good care of you."

And is it my imagination, or do those words send a little shiver down her spine? She's an Omega after all. There are certain reflexes, certain reactions, she just can't help.

"Okay," she says, allowing me to take her hand once again – another action that seems to have her scent spiraling up into the air. "But don't blame me if I bruise your toes or kick your ankles."

"Sure I've come across much worse with horses and cattle, sweetheart," I tell her, pulling her closer, weaving my arm around her waist, and then leading her across to the dance floor.

For a moment we hover on the edge, waiting for the previous dance to come to an end. I keep my hand just where it is, resting on her waist, and to my delight she doesn't wriggle away or step to one side. When the song finishes, I pull her out onto the dance floor, finding a spot for us near the back, because she clearly feels self-conscious.

"What do I do?" she hisses at me as the singer

announces the name of the next song and several girls whoop from the front row.

"The steps are pretty basic," I tell her, and run through them quickly. Her eyes widen again, this time with horror.

"What?" she says. "That was way too quick and way too complicated!"

I show her again, getting her to follow along this time. Although she protests, she picks it up pretty quick. I don't tell her that's only the first few steps – there's at least twenty-odd involved – but then the music's starting and it's too late to back out now.

She steps through the first few confidently enough, but when everyone on the dance floor switches to the right and starts stomping in a different direction, she looks at me in alarm – like a passenger on a sinking ship who's had the last life ring snatched from their grasp.

"It's okay," I say to her. "You'll get the hang of it."

She shakes her head again, gaze darting back to the bar as if, like a scared colt, in a minute she might make a bolt for it.

"I promised to look after you, didn't I, Hollie?" I say.

I thread my arm back around her waist and pull her along with me. Automatically, her shoulders relax.

Okay, the steps are all wrong, and once or twice she does actually stand on my toe – but she's moving in the right direction, not crashing into anyone else. Which is good, because I'm not sure my Alpha instincts could handle this little Omega crashing up close and personal with any other man in this bar.

And soon her shoulders are doing more than relaxing. She's actually leaning into me a little, and a smile's hovering on her lips.

"Enjoying yourself?" I lean closer.

"No," she says, although she's smiling when she says it. "I think this is one of the worst experiences of my life. Worse than the time Annie attempted to take me ice-skating and I took out a family of skaters. Worse than the time Mrs. Hamburg's rottweiler humped my leg so aggressively I had to sedate him. Worse than when my luggage got searched at the airport and when they opened my bag half my under-wear tumbled out everywhere."

I laugh. "You seem to have a habit of landing yourself in trouble."

"You have no idea and if you let go, I'm guaranteed to end up on my ass."

"I won't let go," I growl. "You're safe with me."

It's hot in the bar, especially hot on the tightly packed dance floor, and soon there's a fine sheen of sweat on her neck and shoulders. My own shirt's sticking to my back. It's sending my imagination wild – giving me ideas about sliding my tongue up her neck, tasting that salty flavor that's bound to be lingering there, getting a good lungful of her sweet honey scent.

She's not wrong about having two left feet. The girl's getting most of the steps wrong, and the ones she does get right trail a second or two behind everyone else. Not like the girls in the front row – the ones who come every Friday night in their skimpy jean shorts and even skimpier tops, hips swaying, butts jiggling, every step damn faultless. They're pretty tempting, and if I'm honest, I've been tempted with more than one or two of them.

However – I have to confess – the little Omega getting it all wrong beside me is a hell of a lot more tempting. A hell of a lot. And with my arm wrapped firmly around her waist, I have her moving in the right direction.

That is until we're forced to turn to the right sharply.

She should have two feet on the ground like everyone else, making this move easy. Unfortunately, she's balancing on the toes of her left foot, and the sudden change in direction has her wobbling, toppling, and slipping from my grasp.

She shrieks, arms flapping frantically in the air like an out-of-control windmill. Everyone's gaze snaps our way. Her eyes widen. She looks to me in desperation, and, as if in slow motion, I see her tumbling backwards to the floor.

I dive forward, skidding onto my knees, and catch that girl like she's a football and I'm intercepting a pass. She lands with an oomph in my arms and stares up at me in disbelief as everyone around us breaks into applause.

"Got you," I say with a big grin.

"Got me?!" she squeals. "I nearly landed on my ass like I predicted!"

"You didn't though, did you?" I say, looking down to where her ass is now resting in my lap.

"True," she says, arms around my neck. "Thank you,"

I tip her back up onto her feet and scramble up myself. Everyone's still looking at us, and I frown at them. Some of those front-row girls are giggling.

"Nothing to look at here, folks. Get back to dancing."

I don't need to say it twice – they're all snapping back round.

"I don't know what happened," she says.

"Doesn't matter," I say, shaking my head. "Still having fun?"

She nods with a grin, and off she sets again, stomping her feet, clapping her hands, completely out of time with everyone else. I scurry back to her side, swearing I'll take better care of her this time.

When the song ends, I'm a hell of a lot disappointed about it.

"Wanna stay for another?" I ask her.

"I'm exhausted," she says.

I guess my face must show my disappointment.

"But that was fun. Actually fun," she tells me.

"Actually fun as opposed to ..."

"Mandatory fun."

"Not familiar with that kind of fun."

She makes a face. "Mandatory team-bonding or tedious family-gatherings."

"So nothing pre-determined or obligatory?" She nods. "I've taken note."

I reach for her hand and lead her off the dance floor, but we stand close by, watching the next dance.

"Oh," she says, "the steps aren't that different."

"No," I say. "Once you know the basics, you can pretty much do them all."

She tips back her head and looks up at me. "You dance really well."

"You sound surprised."

"Not many men I've met are willing to dance, let alone are any good at it."

"In a town like this," I tell her, "if you wanted to get a girl, you had to learn to dance."

She raises an eyebrow. "I find it hard to believe you needed to learn to dance to get a girl."

"Oh yeah," I say grinning, pretty pleased with that compliment.

"I mean," she waves her hand in my direction, "you have the whole cowboy thing going on."

"Every dude round here has the cowboy thing going on," I admit. Although I don't admit that me and my pack-mates do it best – I don't want to come across as an arrogant asshole. Not when I like the girl. Not when the girl apparently has a problem with alphas.

"You're from here then?" she asks me.

"Yeah," I say. "Grew up in this town too. Me and Clay have been best friends since kindergarten."

Her face softens, and I take it she thinks that's sweet. I don't mind. I'm happy to gain all the kudos points I can.

I'm about to do some more sweet talking, crack open the classics, when Annie comes pushing through the crowd. She grabs Hollie's hand from mine.

"There you are!" she squeals. "Come on, Travis is making us cocktails!"

And then she's pulling her away, and I wonder how soon it'll be before I can get my hands on that little Omega again.

Chapter Seven

H ollie

Annie has found us a pair of stools by the bar and already has two gigantic cocktails lined up for us with tiny colorful umbrellas and a garnish of fruit.

"You have to try these," she says. "Travis is really talented. They taste amazing."

I nod, realizing just how much of a goner my friend is for the barman. She's always scoffed at pretentious drinks in the past. I take a long suck on my straw.

"Whoa, Annie," I say. "How much alcohol is in that thing?"

"Tonnes," Annie says with a grin, sucking on her own straw. "We're gonna get wasted, Hollie. It's the start of the holidays, no work for freaking ages, and I haven't seen you in even longer."

"Your dad said–"

"My dad always says that. Don't worry about him."

She takes another long draw on her straw, downing the whole cocktail, pushing it to one side, and waving frantically at Travis, who is more than willing to come striding back over to us both.

"Another two, ladies?"

"You bet!" Annie says, and I suck even harder on my straw, attempting to keep up with her.

By the end of our third cocktail, I'm pretty sure all that snow outside has melted and now the bar is floating on a body of water, or else I'm just swaying on my seat. Everything's a little blurry around the edges and I'm finding it hard to keep up with Annie as she gives me the lowdown on everyone in the bar.

"And that's Johnny," she says. "He's the one who rode his horse right inside this bar one time. And over there, that girl, see her, she got caught scratching penises into the paintwork of her ex-boyfriend's prize Cadillac."

I nod along, and Annie's just pointing out someone else in the crowd when she freezes, bouncing up and down on her chair and clapping her hands.

"Oh my goodness, Hollie, do you hear that?"

"Hear what?" I say.

"The song," she says.

I listen carefully. It's a Christmas classic, "All I Want for Christmas Is You."

It's our all-time favorite.

The first Christmas we were in college, we played it non-stop, back to back, singing it as loudly as we could at every opportunity, while clutching hairbrushes and chugging eggnog that came pre-made in cans. It was like our own mini theme song for the holidays.

Annie yanks me off the stool, and then, before I know

what she's doing, she's jumping up onto the bar, pushing away the empty glasses with her boot and signaling me to follow.

"What are you doing?" I shriek.

"It's our favorite song, Hollie, get your ass up here."

Maybe if I hadn't had so many drinks I'd think twice about clambering up onto the bar in my miniskirt in a town where I'm already an outsider and there's a good chance I'll fall off the bar and break my head. But the drink and the alcohol are making everything seem like a fantastic idea tonight, so I don't even hesitate. I scrabble up after my best friend, and soon we both stand together on the bar, arms wrapped around each other, singing our hearts out at the top of our voices.

Probably everyone is looking at us. Then again, I think most of the rest of the bar is singing along to the song too. There's definitely lots of people swaying beneath us. We're just getting to the climax of the song where it gets really high and neither of us can quite make the notes, both of us dissolving into fits of giggles as our voices crack.

When I glance down, there's an angry Alpha standing below us, hands on hips, scowl on his ridiculously handsome face. Clay Jackson. Again. Of course.

He's glaring up at us so fiercely that if I wasn't so drunk I'd be a shaking, blubbering mess. As usual, he looks mightily unimpressed. I hope that isn't because, from this angle, he's peering right up my skirt. I am, after all, wearing my best pair of panties and I had a wax before I left Rockview.

"What the hell are you doing?" he booms above all the music.

"Singing," his little sister says, following it up with a middle finger.

"Get down," he says.

"Nope," she says, shaking her head, clearly delighting in antagonizing her brother.

"You could break your neck," he calls back.

She grins even wider and does a little shuffle along the bar.

Clay's furious gaze finds me next, and, despite the alcohol-soaked state of my blood, I can't help but freeze under the force of it.

"Get down," he barks at me.

He's not my big brother. I'm not his little sister. But I am an Omega and he is an Alpha, and a command like that is instinctively difficult to disobey. My body wants to take a flying jump right off the bar in response to those words – preferably into his waiting arms. But I dig the heels of Mrs. Jackson's lucky cowboy boots into the bar and adopt Annie's brattish persona, mirroring the Alpha with my hands on my hips and shaking my head.

"Do you own this bar?" I ask him.

"No," he says.

"Then I don't think I will."

"You could hurt yourself," he says.

I roll my eyes. He obviously doesn't know that I'm always hurting myself. I've broken my right arm twice, the fingers of my left hand once, and I fractured my cheekbone one time as well. I'm accident prone and nothing is ever going to change that. I've given up trying.

"Fine," the Alpha says, and I expect him to turn around and stomp away in a sulk, leaving Annie and me to our singing. He does the exact opposite. And what he does is so quick – lightning quick – or maybe that's just the drinks again – I don't see it coming. He leaps forward, wraps his arms around my thighs, and then I'm tipping forward and, before I know it, I'm slung over his shoulder and he's marching me straight out of the bar. It's so quick I don't even have time to protest or struggle or wriggle away.

The cold air outside hits me and then my boots are landing in the snow.

"What the hell?" I say. Or perhaps I slur it.

"You're drunk," he says, "and dancing on top of bars is dangerous."

"Flipping people over your shoulder like that is pretty dangerous too, mister," I say, absolutely scandalized.

He snorts. "You weigh half that of a new-born calf!"

Which is most definitely not true. I may be small in height but I'm not one of those slim omegas with model-like figures. I'm all curves and big curves at that.

"Why are you carrying me out of the bar and not your sister?"

"Because," he says, and then falters.

I'm not sure he has a response to that. I tip my head to one side, focusing with all my might on his face because there might now be two of him, two Clay Jacksons standing in front of me. And frankly, one Clay Jackson is more than enough for this world.

A world that spins manically.

I'm wondering if an Alpha really did just sling me over his shoulder and march me out of the bar, or whether this is some crazy drunk-ass dream and I'm gonna wake up back in Rockview any second now.

But unfortunately, it's not a dream, because in the next second, out of nowhere, I feel a strong rumbling in my stomach and I try my best to force it down, but it's no good. And then I'm hurling right by Clay Jackson's smart black cowboy boots, littering chunks of creamy pasta onto the virgin white snow.

He doesn't even jump backwards in alarm. He just stands there watching me with disapproval written all over his face as I vomit into the snow.

When I'm done, I wipe my hand over my mouth and peer up at him.

"Better?" he asks me.

And actually, maybe I am. There's only one of him again now. The world is no longer tipping backwards and forwards on its axis, and it's definitely no longer spinning as quickly as it was a minute ago.

"I'm so sorry," I mumble. "I'll clean your boots for you."

"It's not your fault," he mumbles. "It's Annie's."

"Oh no, it's not," I say. "She just wanted me to have a good time. I haven't had a good time ..."

I trail off, and he looks at me. And then this time it definitely isn't the alcohol, because all of a sudden there are three Alphas standing in front of me. Only this time they aren't duplicates of Clay Jackson. They're his packmates, Nash and Tucker.

"You don't need to get wasted to have a good time," Clay says.

"Gee, Dad," I say. "I know."

Tucker chuckles, his pale green eyes twinkling with mischief. "I don't think he meant it that way, Hollie," he says.

I quirk an eyebrow, because how did he mean it, then?

"I'll get you some water," Clay says, spinning on his heels and marching back toward the bar.

Tucker kicks snow over the lovely pile of vomit I've made and then pulls me to one side, Nash following us.

"What happened?" he asks.

"Cocktails," I say. "Cocktails are what happened."

"Ah," Tucker says with a lopsided smile. "Travis's cocktails are pretty lethal. I'm surprised Annie didn't warn you."

"I think that's what Annie was going for," I say. "Tonight was all about letting my hair down."

"It's been a rough year for you," Nash says sympathetically, as Tucker tucks what is probably a vomit-coated lock of hair behind my ear, and I don't know why or what's happening or if it's the alcohol all over again, but I feel another rumbling inside me and this time it's not creamy pasta vomit, it's a sob. It comes bubbling up into my throat and I can't hold it back, and all of a sudden I'm sobbing into my hands – full-on sobbing, my whole body shaking with it.

"Yes," I splutter. "It's been a really really really tough year."

I'm cold, I'm drunk, I'm far from home. It's Christmas and I really miss my mom. Really really really miss her. An aching gnawing missing her that burrows right down to my bones. All I want is a hug from my mom, but she's not here anymore. She's not here to wrap her arms around me and tell me everything's okay. And that seems truly and brutally unfair.

Except, before I know it, a pair of arms *are* wrapping themselves around me and I'm being pulled into a hug. A great big warm hug that smells of pine forests, cedar, and the open countryside. I'm enveloped in a strong pair of arms and held against a hard, muscular chest.

"Hey," a voice says tenderly, rough stubble grazing my ear. It's Tucker's. "It's okay."

"I'm sorry," I say as I continue to blubber into his shirt, making a nice wet stain that's probably black from my mascara.

"It's alright," he says. "You go ahead. You go ahead and cry. Let it all out, sweetheart."

I do just that. Mostly because I can't help it. Mostly because I haven't had many hugs since my mom died, and not many chances to cry about it either.

Above my sobbing I hear footsteps crunch in the snow and then Clay's voice.

"What's wrong?" he says, with alarm. "What happened?"

"She's sad," Nash explains. "She's had a sad year."

"More likely to be the alcohol," Clay mutters. "I think we ought to take her home."

I tip back my head. All that time and effort I spent on my makeup and my hair, and I'm pretty sure I must look a complete wreck right now. Plus I must smell of vom.

"But what about Annie," I say, "and Mr. J?"

"I expect Annie will be more than happy to get a ride home with Travis," Tucker tells me. Clay snorts somewhere behind him. "And Mr. J will appreciate not having to drive out here in the middle of the night."

I nod. That does sound true. "I'd better check that's okay with Annie first, though," I say. I'm not about to disappear on my best friend, even if she is in the process of hooking up with one seriously hot barman.

Tucker goes to argue, but I shake my head. "It's girl code," I explain.

"Okay," he says. "Can't go against girl code."

"It's absolutely forbidden."

"Totally."

All four of us squeeze our way back into the bar. It's much later now and, although the bar is heaving, it's not quite as busy as it was a couple of hours ago. We find Annie still sitting by the bar, deep in conversation with Travis.

"We're taking Hollie home," Clay tells his sister.

Annie immediately jumps off her seat. "We're going already?" she says.

I take her hands in mine. "No, I'm going," I say. "I'm not feeling so hot. I guess I can't drink like I used to. You stay here." I do the eyes thing that lets her know I'm more than happy for her to stay with the hot barman.

She grins at me and then wraps me in a hug, immediately jumping straight back. "Geez, Hollie, you smell revolting."

"Yeah," I say. "Like I said, the alcohol may not have agreed with me."

"Definitely didn't," Clay mutters.

Annie focuses in on her big brother. "Take good care of her," she says. "No funny business."

"Funny business?" he repeats with disgust.

"She's my friend."

Clay takes a step forward and glares at the barman sitting beside Annie. "Yeah, and she's my little sister," he warns him.

Travis nods. "You know I'll always treat her like a lady."

"Ugh," Annie says. "Please don't. That's the last thing I want."

Clay looks like he might erupt, so it's probably lucky that his pack mate Nash grips his arm and leads him out of the bar, Tucker taking my hand and leading me out too. Soon I'm tucked up in the back of their truck, a blanket wrapped around my lap. And even sooner, I think I'm drifting off asleep, because the next moment I'm being carried out of the truck and up to the house.

"Oh!" I squeal, finding myself tucked up against Tucker's chest once again. "I can walk."

"You looked so cozy. Didn't want to wake you," he tells me.

"Yeah, but it's not a good look, being carried in, is it?" I tell him. "I don't want Mr. and Mrs. Jackson to know how drunk I was. Please don't tell them."

He smiles, places me back on my feet, and pushes open the door. "Sure," he says. "My lips are sealed. You think you can make it up to your room?"

"Absolutely," I say. "I'm feeling so much better." I hesitate. "Thank you."

"You're welcome, Hollie Bright," he tells me.

And I have a feeling that if I hadn't nearly fallen on my ass, embarrassed myself dancing on the bar and vomited in the snow, he would have kissed me.

Chapter Eight

Hollie

I wake up with a splitting great headache and Annie crawling into my bed.

"Did you just get in?" I ask her, spying the morning light creeping in around the curtains.

"Yep," she says, a great big grin on her face, cheeks a rosy red, and smelling like aftershave.

"Did you have fun?" I say as she snuggles up under the covers and we face each other on the bed.

"Lots of fun," she says. "In fact – three lots of fun."

"Three?" I say. "Geez, where'd you get the energy, Annie?"

She kicks me under the covers. "Says an Omega."

"An Omega who hasn't had any action for at least a year, remember?" I tell her. "Anyway, we're not talking about me. We're talking about you. Did you go back to his place?"

"Sure," she says. "We went back to his place, and we went to his truck, and we went..." She pauses, eyes twinkling with mischief, "to the back room of the bar."

"You dirty little thing," I say in pretend outrage, completely delighted for my friend. "Was it hot?"

"Yep, flaming hot," she says, then grimaces. "But I realize I'm also a seriously bad best friend."

"No, you're not."

"I am," she says, doing a little guilty pout. "I took you out dancing on your first night here, then totally ditched you for a guy. That's not what best friends do. I promise to be on my best behavior from now on."

"Annie," I say, "I got drunk, and your big brother had to take me home because I vomited in the snow outside the bar."

"You did?" she says.

"Yep, right by his boots. In fact, I think there were one or two chunks that landed on his toes."

"Ew," Annie says, "but also – great aim. He was such an asshole last night."

"Not really," I say. "He looked after me."

"Too right. It's his duty as my brother," Annie says. "Anyway, let's not talk about my big brother when we're in bed together." I giggle. "How do you feel now?"

I groan. "I feel like my skull's about to split open inside my head."

"Gross," Annie says. "Drink some water and let's go back to sleep."

I fumble around, finding Annie has brought a glass to bed with her. I chug it down, snuggle back up in bed with my best friend, and soon I'm fast asleep.

We're woken several hours later by a knock on the door.

"You girls alive in there?" Mr. J's voice says through the woodwork.

"Just about," Annie replies.

"Would a vegetarian breakfast burrito help you at all?"

"Yes, please," Annie calls out.

"Hash browns?" he asks.

"Obviously," Annie says. "Eggs?"

"What do you take me for? An Amateur?"

"Green chile?" she asks.

"Yep, green chile too – but it's gonna get cold, so get a wriggle on, girls!"

I take a shower, brush my teeth about a billion times, and then find Annie. We make our way back down to the kitchen, Annie reliving some of the more memorable moments from her evening. There's a feast waiting for us on the kitchen table, along with steaming hot coffee and an enthusiastic greeting from both Dolly and Kenny.

I drop onto the nearest chair with a groan, thanking Mr. J with all of my heart. Annie does the same, and we're silent for the next ten minutes as we stuff ourselves with food, down as much coffee as we can and I sneak bits of egg to Dolly under the table. Then we both lean back on our chairs, our tummies most definitely full.

"So," she asks me, "think you can face the day now? How's the head?"

"Much, much better," I say, sipping on my fourth cup of black coffee.

"You know what would help even more – some good old country air?"

I glance toward the window. It's not snowing today, but there's still a thick blanket of it lying on the ground.

"Are we going out riding?" As much as that's my

favorite (if not frequented enough) pastime, I'm not sure I can stomach the idea with a flaming great handover.

"I thought something a little more gentle might be called for," Annie says, probably noting how green my complexion appears this morning.

"Yes, please."

"A leisurely stroll?"

I grimace. I only have my sneakers. And as nice as it was for Mrs. J to lend me her lucky boots, there's no way I'm traipsing through the snow in those. I won't be responsible for ruining them.

"I've got nothing to wear on my feet," I tell my friend.

"That's okay," she says. "We have a billion pairs of snow boots. I'll find something that'll work – and probably an old jacket as well – that would be better than that stupid red one you brought with you."

"Hey," I say.

"Hollie, if you were caught out in a snowstorm wearing that red coat, you'd perish in about a minute flat."

"Fair enough," I say. "But the winter coat choices in Rockview weren't exactly vast."

She nods in understanding. Annie spent the first year of college in Rockview sweltering in the heat, complaining about it non-stop. She really missed the cold weather of Colorado.

We go fumbling through the cupboard with all the spare winter gear and, after a while, find me a suitable pair of boots, some waterproof trousers, and an extra-warm coat. We also pull out a woolly hat and matching mittens.

We wrap ourselves up warm and then head out into the cold, taking a detour to the stables first to say good morning to all the horses and to feed them some carrot-y treats. Then we take a walk around the yard, Annie pointing out the different fields, the different machinery, and the different mountains in the distance.

It's a bright, sunny day, and I have to admit, I like the contrast of the sunshine and the cold – my breath forming little white clouds in front of my face, and my coat warm and snuggly, even though the end of my nose is cold. The bright sunshine reflects off the snow, and it's so beautiful it makes my chest ache.

I wonder how Annie ever had the strength to leave Big Sky Ranch. I know she comes back as often as she can, but I think if I lived here, I'd never want to leave. I don't think I'd even miss the beach. Who needs sand and sea when you can have mountains and snow?

Annie is also right about the fresh air. I can feel my headache melting away, as well as all the embarrassing memories from last night. We link arms like an old married couple, and Annie continues her long description of the events from last night as we walk across the snowy fields.

"I'm telling you, Hollie, the man has such hard abs you could chop wood on them – and possibly the most beautiful dick I've ever seen in my entire life." She sighs dramatically. "In fact, the whole man is just completely, spectacularly, jaw-droppingly beautiful."

I make a little face, and my best friend catches me do it from the corner of her eye.

"What?" she says, obviously a little insulted. "You don't think he's hot?"

"Oh no," I say, "completely, totally hot – and totally your type."

Annie's always gone for the bad-boy types with all the tattoos and piercings in strange places.

"Then what was with your face?" she says, not letting it go.

"It's just," I pause, "I can appreciate a fine set of abs and even a beautiful cock." Annie nods in agreement. "But you have to admit, there are certain parts of a man's anatomy that aren't so pleasant to look at."

Annie tilts her head to one side. "Go on," she says.

"Well," I say, "the asshole, for starters."

Annie laughs. "You don't find an asshole attractive?"

"No," I shake my head. "I know that's some people's thing, but for me, it's always looked a bit – well, puckered."

Annie laughs even harder. "Is that it? Or are there any other parts?"

"Toes," I say. "I can't stand strangely long toes. And also, balls."

Annie gasps. "Balls? I love a pair of balls!"

I pull another face. "They're just so funny-looking," I say. "Some especially so – they look like ... wrinkled old walnuts."

Annie laughs even harder, so hard she's forced to stop walking and bend over, clutching her stomach.

"Oh my goodness. I'm done with you, Hollie," she says. "I'm never going to be able to crack a set of nuts again."

"What kind of nuts are we talking about here?" I ask her as she roars even louder.

"The kind you eat!"

"Still not helping," I say, because I know my friend has a penchant for sucking on a pair of balls.

"Never mind," Annie says, straightening and wiping at her eyes with her gloves. "What do you want to do now?"

I peer out across the snow-covered landscape and then look back at my friend.

"There is one thing," I say, "but maybe..." I trail off.

"What is it, Hollie?" she asks.

"This is only my second time in snow, right?" Annie nods. "And the first time, it was slushy and wet and no good. Which means I've never ..."

"You've never?" Annie asks.

"Built a snowman."

Annie jumps back in horror. "Never?" she asks.

I shake my head. "Never," I say. "I'm a snowman virgin."

"Oh my goodness," Annie says, putting her hands on her hips, "that is something we must address even more urgently than the sex drought."

I nod my head enthusiastically.

"Hollie do you ..." she breaks into song, "wanna build a snowman?"

I nod even more enthusiastically, and Annie taps her chin. "Let me think – where would be the best place to build it? I think back at the house. Then we've got access to hats and scarves and all the other paraphernalia we need. Holy shit, Hollie, we are going to make the best damn snowman in the history of the earth!"

I smile back at her. "Yes, please."

Twenty minutes later, we're rolling big boulders of snow around the front yard. The snow catches on the ball and it increases in size with every roll until we have a body that reaches up to my middle and a head that makes the snowman about my height.

"Not bad," Annie says, standing back and brushing snow off her gloves. "Now we just need to decorate him."

"And name him," I say.

"Name comes after we've finished decorating him," Annie explains. "I've got to understand what his personality is like first."

I nod in agreement.

"Stay here," she says, and runs up into the house.

While I'm waiting, I pat down the Snowman's body and head, smoothing and perfecting the snow. Annie returns with a basket full of different things – there's a cowboy hat, a scarf, another pair of mittens, a carrot, and two walnuts.

She hands those straight to me, and I lift them up, one in each hand.

"See what I mean?" I say. "There really isn't very much difference."

Annie raises an eyebrow. "I think the man drought has lasted so long, Hollie Bright," she tells me, "that you've forgotten what certain things look like."

I shake my head. "Certain images cannot be erased from my memory," I say. "I couldn't forget even if I wanted to."

"Ew," Annie gags. "Then you've definitely been dating the wrong men."

"So, what are we using these for? The eyes?"

Annie grins manically, snatches the walnuts from my hands, and positions them fairly centrally in the body of the snowman. Then she grabs the carrot from the basket and adds it too.

I can't help bursting out laughing. "I didn't know we were building an X-rated snowman."

"We're building our perfect man," she says, "although..." She considers the carrot. "Could do with a couple of extra inches."

I take a look. "Yeah," I say, "definitely. A couple of extra inches."

Next, we wind the scarf around the snowman's neck, add the cowboy hat, use some stones we find for the eyes, some sticks for the arms, and another carrot for the nose.

"Jeez," I say. "I think Mr. Snowman's nose is bigger than his dick."

"Poor Mrs. Snowman," Annie says.

"What the hell is that?" a deep voice sounds behind us, making the two of us jump guiltily.

We were so engrossed in our snowman-making, we never heard the three Alphas creeping up behind us, who are now examining our work with curiosity.

I can't help blushing. "We've been building a snowman," Annie says, "because Hollie was a snowman virgin."

My cheeks burn even hotter.

"Mom isn't going to like that obscenity standing right outside the house," Clay says.

"Who says it's an obscenity?" Annie asks. "It's a piece of art."

All of our gazes fall to Mr. Snowman's genitalia.

"If that's your best artistic interpretation, I'm wondering if you girls have ever been close to a man's junk before," Tucker says.

"Yeah, it's rather on the small side," Nash adds.

"You can do better, then, hey, Tucker Parker?" Annie asks.

Tucker winks at her. "If you wanna take a look, Annie Jackson, you can make that judgment yourself."

Clay punches him in the arm hard enough to make him grunt, and Annie reaches down, takes a handful of snow, pats it into a ball, and tosses it straight at Tucker's face.

"Stop harassing us," she says. "This is very important work."

Tucker ducks, and the snowball goes sailing over his head, hitting her brother straight in the face instead.

I can't help but giggle as he wipes the snow from his eyes and glares at his sister.

"Oh no, you didn't," he says.

Annie takes a step backward. "I was aiming at Tucker.".

"You missed," Clay tells her.

They're so busy glaring at each other, neither spots Tucker duck down, make a snowball of his own, and throw it straight at Annie. It hits her on the shoulder and she screeches in outrage.

Then all hell breaks loose. Annie's scrabbling on the ground for more snow as the three Alphas do the same.

"Hollie!" Annie yells. "Don't just stand there – help me!"

I've never made a snowman before, and I've never made snowballs, but I was pretty good at baseball as a kid – and my aim, unlike the rest of my coordination, is pretty darn good.

I scoop up snow and start tossing it at the three Alphas, following Annie's example. At the same time, snowballs start flying my way. I dodge a couple, but a couple more hit me on the top of my head and one on the arm.

Then Annie's screaming at me to retreat behind Mr. Snowman for protection. We run that way, cowering behind him and using his body as a shield as we continue to toss snowballs their way.

I wasn't lying about my aim – I manage to hit Clay right smack in the face again, Tucker on the jaw, and Nash right in the middle of his chest.

Hidden behind the snowman, they're finding it a lot harder to hit us – but that doesn't last long, because soon Tucker's calling for a charge and they're sprinting toward us.

Annie's pulled from behind the snowman by Tucker, who drags her down into the snow, as her brother holds a snowball in his hand ready to smush it straight into her face.

"Surrender, little sister," he says.

"Hey!" I shout at him. "This is cheating!"

"The rules of snowball fights are:" Tucker tells me, "there are no rules."

"Do you surrender?" Clay asks his little sister once again.

She glares up at him.

"Never!" I scream, and then I'm running toward him and leaping straight up onto his back, shoving ice-cold snow right down the neck of his shirt.

He jolts in surprise, loses his balance, and then the two of us are tumbling down into the snow together. Somehow, in the confusion, the great big Alpha lands right down on top of me.

We're staring at each other, nose to nose.

It's the closest I've been to a man while vertical in longer than a year.

It's the closest I've been to an Alpha while vertical in forever.

Chapter Nine

C lay

I don't know how I find myself lying on top of Hollie Bright, but I don't hate it. I don't hate it at all. Up close, her scent is even sweeter. Her eyes a formidable turquoise color and her breath warm against my skin. Our mouths are only inches apart, and it would be exceptionally easy to lower my head and press my lips to her soft pink ones, glossy with some kind of balm.

However, not only do we have an audience, not only has Hollie Bright made no indication whatsoever that she'd like me to kiss her, she's also my little sister's best friend, a best friend who has come for a week of recuperation and not a week of frolicking. A fact I seem to have to be constantly reminding myself of over the last 24 hours.

"Jeez, Hollie, are you okay?" my little sister calls out.

"Oh," Hollie says, those mesmerizing eyes gazing

straight into mine as she bites on her bottom lip. "Yeah, I'm fine."

"But," I say, "I seem to have the upper hand now, Omega."

I don't mean to say that word; it just slips out of my mouth, and I notice the way it causes her pupils to blossom.

Just an innate, pre-programmed reaction she can't control. And yet, a reaction that calls to all my own innate, pre-programmed reactions.

"Upper hand how?" she says, with a hint of defiance.

I scoop up a load of snow and hold it above her face.

"You wouldn't dare," she says, although I can tell by the wobble in her voice that she's not so sure about that.

"I wouldn't?" I say.

"I'd like to remind you, Clay Jackson," she says, "that I'm a guest in your house, that I've only been in the neighborhood for a day, and it wouldn't be very polite to shove snow in my face."

"Even though you just shoved snow down my shirt?" I ask.

"Hmm," she manages a little shrug.

"Even though you vomited on my boots last night?"

"I missed your boots," she says.

I shake my head. "There was also that time—"

"Okay, Okay," she says. "I surrender." She closes her eyes. "Do your worst."

But the problem is, with her eyes closed like that, she looks even more kissable. Everything in my body is urging me to do it. Most of all, it's her scent urging me; there's all these little signals in it that are activating my Alpha hind-brain, telling me to *Kiss the Omega, kiss the Omega, kiss the Omega.*

That can't be right. There's no way Hollie Bright wants

me to kiss her. There's no way she wants *an Alpha* to kiss her. That can't be what her scent is signaling.

So it's going to have to be the snow instead.

Except, I'm not so sure I can bring myself to do that.

Reluctantly – because I'm a creep –I roll myself up off the Omega.

Her eyes snap open, and she looks up at me with curiosity.

When I'm standing up, I drop the snowball to the floor and offer her my hand, meaning to pull her up onto her feet. She lifts her hand, but before I get a chance to take it, I'm ambushed by two pack mates and a little sister. They come at me from all directions, smothering snow in my face, in my hair, and once again down my shirt, and then somehow all of us are wrestling in the snow.

And I try not to think about how much I'd like to be wrestling with the Omega in my bed.

The wrestling continues for 10 minutes until we realize that my mom is yelling at us. We all stop, glancing up from the ground to find her standing by the snowman that Hollie and Annie were building. She's looking mighty unim-pressed.

"What is this monstrosity?" she asks.

"Annie built it," I say.

"Annie Jackson," my mom says, "I thought we educated you better than that."

She snaps out the carrot and the two walnuts from the middle of the snowman's belly, lowering it half a foot, and rearranging them.

"There," she says, "that's much more anatomically correct. Seems you need to go back to school."

We all laugh. And then my mom is saying, "we're leaving for the tree in 20 minutes, so anyone who needs to change clothes, visit the bathroom, or grab equipment – go now. We're not waiting for you."

"Tree?" Hollie asks as she climbs up onto her feet and brushes snow from her body. An action I'd happily do for her.

"Yep," Annie says, "it's a Jackson tradition. The day before Christmas Eve we head out to the Christmas tree nursery, choose one we like, and bring it in."

"Christmas tree nursery?" Hollie asks.

"Yeah," I explain. "We grow a few Christmas trees here on the ranch. Not very many, just enough for the locals."

"And enough to ensure we have a good choice of the best for ourselves," Annie says. "Come on."

She beckons to her friend, and then they're skipping off to the house. I climb slowly back onto my feet as my pack mates do the same.

"You looked very comfortable," Tucker says, landing his hand on my shoulder with a big grin.

"I don't know what you mean," I say.

"I think you do," he says, his grin widening further. "Landing on top of the Omega like that. I'd have paid a lot of money to swap places with you."

"It was an accident," I explain. "She could have been hurt."

"She looked very comfortable from where I was standing too," Tucker says.

I glance at him, wondering if he's saying that to wind me up or if it's really true. But Nash is nodding in agreement.

"Her scent seemed to suggest she liked it as well."

So he noticed that too.

"It's just an Omega reaction," I say. "Hollie Bright's never liked me, and she's definitely never liked Alphas."

"Why wouldn't she like you?" Nash asks seriously.

"Yeah," Tucker says, "You've got the personality of a broom. You're as grumpy as Scrooge and you like to berate her in public."

"He's also tolerably good looking, hard working, and loyal," Nash says.

I ignore them both, heading instead to where my truck is parked outside the house.

"Come on," I say. "Let's get a head start on the others. Let's choose the best tree."

I almost say for Hollie, because the seriously soft spot I've always harbored for the omega – the one that has lain dormant for years – is beginning to reawaken, even if she did vomit on my boots last night. I want her to have the best Christmas because I know it's going to be hard for her and I want to make it special.

We drive out to the copse of Christmas trees. We cut and shipped out most of the fully grown trees several weeks back, but we left about half a dozen of the best for the family to choose from. We walk through them now, assessing each one. Nash, in particular, has a strong opinion on Christmas tree aesthetics. He insists it can't be too tall, too short, too fat, or too thin, and he likes it to look symmetrical.

"I think it's out of these two," he says.

"It doesn't matter what you think," I say. "You know it's going to be my mom's choice."

The other two nod in agreement. They spent last Christmas here at the ranch with my family as well and they know how things work.

Five minutes later, my dad's truck is pulling up, and he climbs out along with my mom, Hollie, and Annie. They walk into the copse of trees. As well as the six fully grown, there are the ones we planted more recently – all different heights.

Hollie's eyes light up. "It is so pretty," she says. "And there's so many Christmas trees."

"And we've come to choose the best," my dad explains. "The one we're going to put in the front room."

"This is so lovely," Hollie says. "We never had a real Christmas tree at home before."

"Oh no," Annie says, "don't tell me you had one of those horrible plastic ones."

"There's no point in having a real tree in Rockview," Hollie reminds her. "It's so hot, they wither in about three seconds flat."

"Well, this one will last," my mom says. "So come on, Hollie, help us choose."

She leads the Omega through to the remaining fully grown trees, and they walk through, my sister on the other side of my mom. We watch from a distance as the women assess each tree.

"We could be here a while," my dad reminds us men, passing me the family axe.

"I think they'll choose that one," Nash says, pointing to the one he's already selected.

The girls continue to weave in and out of the trees, Hollie's voice and her scent carrying back to us on the cold air and making something in my stomach warm and cozy. Then they're walking back toward us.

"Chosen?" my dad asks them.

"It's out of two," Annie says.

And Nash smiles, because it seems his prediction was correct.

"I think Hollie should choose," my mom says.

"Me?" Hollie says. "It's your family tree. It's your house, your tradition."

"Yes," my mom says, "and you're our guest, so I'd like you to choose."

Hollie spins back round and looks across at the small selection of trees.

"It feels a bit cruel," she says.

"Don't tell me you have a problem with cutting down trees as well," I mutter.

"No, I mean each one was grown to fulfill its Christmas destiny as a Christmas tree, and only one gets to fulfill that destiny. What will happen to the rest?"

"We'll cut them down and use them for firewood most probably," I say.

The Omega practically balks in front of us.

"We could have two trees," Tucker says, and I glare at him, because two trees is twice the work. It's hard enough as it is cutting down one tree.

"No, I can choose," Hollie says. She taps her fingers against her plush pink lips. "That one," she says at last, picking exactly the tree that Nash had already chosen.

"Good choice," he says.

"That tree it is," I say, swinging the axe up onto my shoulder and marching that way.

"What?" she says. "Aren't you going to cut it down with a chainsaw?"

"Absolutely not," my dad says. "Got to do it the old-fashioned way, the way this family has been doing it for decades."

"You're really going to cut it down by hand?" she says. "Isn't that going to take hours?"

I snort. "No," I say, striding to the tree, aware that the little Omega is trotting along beside me. "Stand back," I tell her, and then I'm swinging the axe through the air. The blade hits the tree trunk with a loud thwack, making the Omega gasp. I do it again, and her scent spirals through the air. I peek her way. I take it she likes this display, and so I put on my best show for her, rolling up my sleeve, tossing my hat to one side, and flexing my biceps.

I said I wanted to make her happy and if watching me swing my axe does just that, who am I to complain.

Chapter Ten

Hollie

Every girl has that thing that does it for them. For some, it's watching men do press-ups at the gym. For others, it's watching firefighters wield gigantic hoses or watching football players tackle one another into the ground.

I hadn't quite appreciated that, for me, it's watching grown men swing axes through the air. But it's hot. Seriously hot. So hot, I'm surprised I'm not gushing slick everywhere.

Clay Jackson isn't even topless. He's wearing several layers of clothing, and yet the way he grunts, the way his muscles flex, the way he handles the axe – I think I may actually melt into a puddle right here and now.

The tree is big, and the trunk is surprisingly thick, and yet it takes him probably a dozen hits with the axe before the thing is wavering.

"Stand back," he calls.

Then he's walking up to the tree, pushing against the trunk, and with an almighty groan the tree topples and lands in the snow. Everybody gives an appreciative clap, and then his pack mates are stepping forward, and together they're lifting the tree onto their shoulders.

I have to admit that that is also insanely hot. I've unlocked a new kink, and when I'm safely back in Rockview, I'll probably be searching for videos of men chopping down trees as my nighttime entertainment for the rest of the year.

The men throw the tree into the back of their truck, and then we're all climbing back inside and driving to the house.

"How did you find that?" Mrs. J asks me from the front seat.

I'm very glad she can't see my face – or, for that matter, read all the dirty thoughts in my head.

"That was fun," I squeak.

And I swear Annie senses something funny going on with me, because she narrows her eyes my way.

"I love all these family traditions," I add.

"Yes," Mrs. J says. "Although I wish the boys would use the chainsaw and the correct safety equipment. It gives me a slight heart attack every year when they do it this way."

I know what she means. I think I was on the verge of a heart attack myself. But I just murmur my agreement and avoid my best friend's gaze, choosing to stare out the window instead.

When we arrive back at the house, the men are already carrying the tree up the steps and inside. Mrs. J has a pot filled with sand waiting for the tree, and the men position it down inside and spend the next few moments ensuring it's not only secure but straight. Nash, in particular, seems to think it's important that the tree looks its best.

Then we all stand back and admire it, shooing Kenny away as he attempts to nibble on a branch.

"Right," Mrs. J says. "Now that's done, you kids can get busy decorating it."

"Aren't you helping too?" I ask.

"Oh no," she says. "We're making the snacks."

And with that, Mr. and Mrs. Jackson disappear off to the kitchen.

"I really hope," Annie says with an eye roll, "that making snacks isn't a euphemism for something else."

"Please do not be disgusting," her brother says.

"What?" Annie says innocently. "I think it's nice that our parents still have a sex life."

Clay glares at his little sister, grabbing a load of tinsel from the box on the floor and walking right round to the other side of the tree.

I pick out some pretty baubles from the box, letting Dolly steal a plastic ball-shaped one from my hands and take it away for a chew, and begin to hang them on the lower branches of the tree. Decorating the tree like this was a tradition that me and my mom had too. We'd put on our pajamas and a load of Christmas music, crack open some store-bought mulled wine and a box of cookies, and decorate the tree while dancing around, singing as well.

It was one of my favorite moments of Christmas. Just me and my mom, having fun. And as lovely as it is to be here with Annie and her family in this beautiful place, as welcome as they've made me feel, I can't help the ache that starts to develop in my chest.

I guess it was inevitable that the sadness would hit me at

some point. I just didn't expect it to come on so quickly. Or so violently.

I hang the last bauble in my hand and then go tap my best friend on her shoulder.

"I'm just going up to my room for a bit," I tell her.

"Are you okay?" Annie says. "Has the hangover returned?"

"No," I say. "It's not that. It's just..." I trail off.

But I don't need to say the words. My best friend knows me well enough.

"I just need a moment or two to myself."

"Absolutely." Annie wraps me in a hug. "I understand. But if you want company or you want to talk or you just want to—"

"It's fine, Annie," I tell her. "I just need a moment or two by myself."

I walk out of the giant family living room, passing the kitchen where I can hear Mr. and Mrs. Jackson laughing loudly, creep up the stairs, and into the bedroom that's mine for the next few days. I shut the door behind me and slump down onto the bed, snuggling under the covers and pulling them right up to my chin.

I close my eyes. I know my mom wouldn't want me to be sad. In fact, her last coherent words to me were to be happy, to enjoy my life. And I'm trying my best. I really am. But it's so hard sometimes. Especially when I want to talk to her. Especially when I want to laugh with her. Especially when I just want to send her silly memes of hot men chopping down trees.

I close my eyes. What I hate most is it's becoming harder and harder to remember her face. It was something that was always so familiar, and now, the more I try to reach for it in my mind, the more blurry and distorted it becomes.

"I miss you, Mom," I whisper. "But I'm going to try. I'm going to try to be happy."

I don't know how long I lie in bed, but the room is dark when there's a knock on the door. I expect it's Annie, come to check up on me.

"Come in," I say.

When the door opens, I'm surprised to find it's not my best friend, but my best friend's mom. She shuts the door behind her and tiptoes across the room, coming to sit on the bed as I sit up.

"You okay, honey?" she asks. "You doing all right?"

"I'm sorry," I say. "I don't mean to be rude or–"

"Nonsense." She shakes her head. "You take all the time you need. I just wanted to check on how you were doing, that's all."

"I'm doing okay," I tell her. "It's just hard sometimes."

"Of course it is," she says. "But you know, lying around on your own in the dark probably makes it seem a whole lot worse."

I nod. I know she's right.

"I don't know if Annie ever told you, but we lost a child. Before we had Clay."

"I'm so sorry," I tell her.

"So I know what it's like, Hollie. I know how overwhelming the grief can be. It swallows you up until you feel like you're drowning in it. And no matter how hard you fight, no matter how hard you struggle, there are times when you find yourself sinking – sinking to the bottom. But the thing is," she continues, "you've got to keep fighting it. You've got to keep struggling. You've got to keep swimming against it. Find the thing that brings you joy and cling to it like a life raft. So what is that, Hollie?"

"The things that bring me joy?"

"Yes. Home-baked cookies? Dancing on bars?"

"You heard about that, huh?"

"Clay's a good boy. He always tells his mom," she says with a grin. "So, is that what it is?"

I shake my head. "Animals – animals always cheer me up." Looking after the animals in the veterinary clinic has been the thing that's kept me surviving over the last few months. Cuddles with kittens or playtime with doggies stops all the sadness, like a plug in a leaky dam. "I'd really like to go see the horses again."

"Horses are one thing we can definitely do. Come on then."

She takes me downstairs, and we find my best friend sitting cross-legged in front of the Christmas tree, piles of presents, wrapping paper, and Sellotape scattered all around her. The tree's all decorated and lit up now, and in the dark room it looks so pretty, for a moment, I just stand and stare.

"Don't worry," I say, leaning into Mrs. J's arm. "The horses can wait. Annie's clearly in the middle of something."

"Clearly," Mrs. J says, but she doesn't let go of my hand, pulling me toward the kitchen instead. "Don't worry, we'll find someone else to take you out to the horses."

Mr. J has an apron tied around his middle and is supervising several simmering pots on the stove.

"Where's one of those boys when you need them?" Mrs. J says, her hand still clasped to mine as she pulls me outside of the house now and down the porch steps.

We find them out the front, loading round hay bales onto their truck. If I thought the wood chopping was hot, I realize throwing giant bales of hay is just as hot. I need to come back in the summer when all these men will almost definitely be topless while they undertake these tasks.

"Clay!" Mrs. J calls. "Can I steal Nash for a moment?"

Her son lowers the hay bale he has clasped in his hands and peers over toward us. His eyes flick from his mom to me, then back again, and he gives a short, sharp nod. Nash throws another hay bale into the truck, wipes his sleeve over his brow, and comes striding over to us.

"How can I help?" he asks us both.

"I think the horses need grooming," Mrs. J says. "Hollie's willing to help. But maybe you could show her how we do it round here?"

She gives me a little push toward Nash, making it clear that I'm not going to get a chance to back out from this.

"Let's go then," Nash says.

He's striding to the barn in the next moment, and I have no choice but to trot along beside him.

"She likes you," Nash tells me as I drag the brush down Cloud's long, soft neck.

"I like her too," I say. "She has such a lovely nature."

"Not always," Nash says. "This one can be a bit feisty, but I think you're a calming influence on her. Or ..." he trails off, adjusting his glasses as he does.

"Or?" I say.

He looks at me. "This one has a penchant for sugar cubes. Definitely has a sweet tooth. And your scent, well..."

"Oh," I say, trying my best to suppress the smile that comment brings. "Some people find my scent a little too sweet," I say. Sickly is the word I remember one of the guys I dated describing it.

Nash snorts. "It's just the right amount of sweet, in my opinion. And I have a reputation for being particularly picky about these things."

"You do?" I say.

"Yeah. They say I'm a perfectionist." He shrugs, continuing to pick out Cloud's hooves.

And I wonder what has happened to my brain, because this is not the same as cutting trees, or swinging axes, or throwing hay bales – and yet this is just as hot.

Or maybe, I have to admit, it's not the actions. It's the Alphas themselves.

I've avoided Alphas because the ones I met back in Rockview – the ones I went on a couple of dates with when I first presented as an Omega – were rude, obnoxious, and incredibly pushy. It was clear that all they wanted was to get inside my panties as quickly as possible.

And me, a young Omega, a complete hormonal mess, didn't want that at all. After all, my mom had been left high and dry herself by an Alpha – young, single, in her early twenties. As much as I love my mom, as much as I loved my childhood, I knew it had been incredibly hard on her, supporting the two of us with no one to lean on, no one to help. And I definitely didn't want to end up the same way.

The thing is, the Betas I've dated didn't turn out to be much better. A lot of them were giant jerks too, which is one of the reasons I've been off men for the last year and a bit. That, and I was too busy caring for my mom.

"Perfection, huh?" I say to him. "That's a high standard to maintain."

"I always say," he tells me, his eyes flicking up to meet mine, "that if a job's worth doing, it's worth doing well."

And why does that send a shiver down my spine? Why do I think there's hidden meaning in those words?

"Especially when it comes to my girls," he says, patting Cloud's rump.

And I'm definitely losing my mind, because that sends another shiver down my spine. A man who cares for his animals has always sent my pulse spiraling. It's lucky most of the other vets at the clinic are women or married – otherwise I'd have fallen in love with them all.

"I understand what you mean," I tell him. "I always want to do my best for my patients as well."

Mrs. J is right. My spirits lift as I continue to groom Cloud, lost in the repetition of it, in the smell of the horse and the scent of the Alpha and in his deep voice as he asks me questions about my job, about my life in Rockview – and lastly, about my mom.

I didn't think I'd want to talk about her, not after the attack of the sadness. But actually, I find it helps. I guess I haven't talked about her with anyone for months now.

"She was young when she had me," I explain. "And I think, although that made it hard for her, it was really special for me. She had a great imagination, lots of energy. She was always swapping jobs, trying her hand at this, trying her hand at that. She never gave up trying to make a better life for herself or for me."

"She sounds like an incredible woman, Hollie," Nash says. "And I think she must have been to have brought up a remarkable woman like you."

I smile into the horse's coat. "She always said I was the best thing she ever did. Her greatest creation. Her proudest moment."

He nods. "That's the biggest compliment."

"It is," I say. "I wish I could be more like her."

He stops what he's doing and looks over at me again.

"The two of you sound remarkably alike," he says. "I'm surprised you'd say that."

"Oh no, she was wonderful," I say. "And I'm... well." I make a face. "I vomited on Clay's boots last night and I almost broke his neck out there in the snow."

"Yes," Nash says with a smile. "It was brilliant. Clay could do with a bit more chaos in his life."

I rest my hand on my hip. "Are you saying I'm chaotic, Nash?"

"Absolutely. Absolutely chaotic." He grins. "Chaotic perfection."

Chapter Eleven

H ollie

"It's Christmas Eve Eve," Annie announces, skipping into my room the next morning, "and I have plans. So get your ass out of bed, chica, and come have some breakfast. Dad's making pancakes."

"Your dad is a saint," I say. "Do you think he'd move to Rockview and become my own personal chef?"

"Nope," Annie says, spinning on her toes and skipping straight out of the room again. "Be downstairs in 15 minutes."

My spirits are feeling much brighter this morning, and I emerge from my bed with a big smile on my face. I think that's probably partly to do with all the beautiful scenery here on Big Sky Ranch. And to be clear, when I say scenery, I'm talking Alphas. I can't help thinking about the tree chopping, the bale throwing, and the horse grooming. Plus, my conversation with Nash keeps floating into my head. I've never met a man like that before – straight-talking and yet sensitive. And Tucker – he makes me laugh in a way I haven't done for months. And then there's Clay. I still haven't made my mind up about him. But I remind myself as I head for the shower and decide I ought to select the coldest setting: I'm not here to gawk at Alphas. I'm here to spend time with my best friend. A best friend who's waiting for me downstairs.

Once I'm dressed, I set off out of my door to find Dolly the dog and Kenny her shadow, the rabbit, both sitting on the landing.

"Well, hello there," I say to them both. "Good morning to you and a happy Christmas Eve Eve." I bend down and tickle first Dolly under the chin and then stroke along Kenny's ears. They both clearly enjoy the attention. Dolly's tail starts wagging furiously, and I continue to tell them both how beautiful they are as I oblige them with further chin scratches.

That is until I hear a loud cough behind me and the smell of pine fills my nostrils. I curl back up and spin around to find Tucker standing right behind me with his trademark grin plastered across his face. I realize that's because I'm wearing my tight jeans today and, folded over like that, I just gave him a very clear view of my ass. If the smile on his face is any indication, he seemed to appreciate it.

"That's one way to brighten my morning," he says with a wink.

"I agree," I tell him, pretending not to understand. "What more could you want than a greeting from these two?" I point at the rabbit and the dog.

"They're cute," he agrees, "but neither has an ass like yours."

I don't know whether to slap him round the face or burst into a fit of giggles. I decide to adopt a fake outrage.

"I assure you," I tell him, "my ass is nowhere near as cute as Dolly's or Kenny's. It's not fluffy, for starters."

"Good to know," Tucker answers. "Where are you heading to? You lost?"

"Nope," I say. "Heading down for breakfast. Mr. J's made pancakes this morning."

"Then I think I may have to make a little detour," he says.

We walk down the stairs together and I try my best not to inhale his fresh pine scent or notice how in sync our steps seem to be or recall how good his arm felt wrapped around my waist when we were dancing.

"How did you sleep?" he says.

"Like a log. It's so quiet out here. The traffic in Rockview's insane. There's always a siren blaring or a horn blasting. I didn't realize how noisy it was until this visit."

"Yeah," he says. "It's one of the things I like most about this place – open space, the tranquility – so damn peaceful."

"Don't you miss excitement?" I say.

"Trust me," he says, "trying to herd several hundred head of cattle gives me all the excitement I need."

"So you're a real cowboy," I say.

"You bet, sweetheart. One hundred percent."

This time I do giggle, which has my best friend swinging around and staring at me as we walk into the kitchen together.

"Where did you spring from, Tucker Parker?" she asks him with a suspicious look.

"Had to go get something from the attic," he says, patting his jacket pocket.

"Hmm," Annie says, obviously not quite convinced by his explanation.

He takes a seat with us at the kitchen table. "Then I heard about pancakes," he tells her.

"There may not be enough for you," Annie says.

"There's plenty," Mr. J says, flipping one down on my plate and another on Tucker's.

Tucker immediately starts piling his pancake with syrup, cream, and choc chips.

"Oh my goodness," I say, "that will seriously rot your teeth."

"You'll be happy to know, Hollie, I own all my own teeth." He draws back his lips to show off two rows of white, straight teeth. "And it's Christmas. Plus, I've got a hard, hard day's work ahead of me. I need all the sugar I can get."

"You're working today, even though it's Christmas Eve Eve?" I ask.

"Absolutely," he says. "Work never stops on the ranch."

Annie nods in agreement.

I sprinkle my own pancake with some bananas and smear some peanut butter over the top. I haven't eaten something like this in years.

"So what are these big plans you have for us today?" I ask my best friend.

"We're heading into town to do a little more gift buying."

"You need to buy yet more presents? Annie, you wrapped about a hundred last night."

"Yes, but there are still one or two little things I need to get."

"What you have to understand about Annie," her dad

says, "is that she prides herself on being a present-buying, gift-giving expert."

"*The* expert," Annie corrects. "I buy the best gifts ever."

I nod. I have to agree. My best friend has always given me the most thoughtful, lovely little gifts for as long as I've known her.

"Which," Annie continues, "drives my big brother nuts."

"Nuts? How come?"

"Because he's absolutely awful at choosing gifts. Like, the worst. Which means he always feels incredibly guilty when I buy him these thoughtful, incredible presents and he buys me trash. *Which* means, because he feels so guilty, he's nice to me for at least the first three months of the year."

"That is so damn crafty, Annie," Tucker says, shaking his head with obvious admiration.

"I'm the little sister," Annie says. "It's in the job description."

Once we've finished our breakfast, I wrap myself back up in that warm coat and those snow boots, and we pile into Annie's truck. It's the first time I've been in her truck, and now I understand why her brother was so reluctant to let her drive it out to the airport. It's ancient, rusty in several places, and it takes her three turns of the key before the engine starts rumbling away. It splutters and coughs like an old man suffering with pneumonia.

"Annie, is this truck going to make it into town?" I say with apprehension.

"She's never let me down yet," Annie says confidently.

"Why don't you get a new one?" I mutter.

"Because I'm loyal, Hollie Bright," she says. "As you know. That's why I didn't dump you as a best friend when you forgot to pass on that message from Professor Woo and I nearly failed her class, or that time you spilled red wine all down my white dress when we were at that seriously glitzy party."

"I'm also loyal," I remind her. "That's why I haven't dumped *you* for ditching me at the bar two nights ago."

"Fair," Annie says, pulling on the old shift stick and jerking us away along the track.

It's a million times bumpier than it was in Mr. J's truck or in Clay's, but I have to admit the old girl does have some character to her. Annie points out the different properties as we pass other ranches and then explains which family lives where and who owns what. We pass some people out horseback riding. And then we're rumbling into town. She parks up on Main Street and announces that we're going to the hardware store.

I whistle. "Gee whiz, Annie, you're taking my virginity at every opportunity you can."

"Don't tell me," she says. "You've never stepped inside a hardware store before."

"Yeah," I say. "Never have."

"What have you done when you've needed to fix a leaky tap or hang up a painting?"

"I've called someone to do it for me."

"Oh, Hollie," she says. "That is pathetic."

I shrug. "I have certain skills, and DIY is not one of them."

"Certain skills, huh?" Annie says, waggling her eyebrows. "Care to elaborate?"

"Nope," I say. "Let's go examine the tools."

Annie is after something in particular for her dad, and soon she's in conversation with the owner, so I browse around the shop while they're chatting, amazed that there could be so many different shapes and sizes of nails and screws. Honestly, can't you just use the same thing for everything?

When Annie has what she needs, she collects me and we head for the door.

"This used to be my brother's favorite shop when he was growing up," she says. "He used to save all his pocket money to come here."

I peek back over my shoulder. "I find that hard to believe," I say. "What could he possibly spend his pocket money on – 10,000 different screws?"

Most teenage boys I knew would have spent their money on video games or, let's face it, porn.

"He likes to build things," Annie explains. "He always has. He was always making dens in the forest for us. He built us a tree house all by himself. That cabin they're staying in now – he built that too. And he's going to build the house, eventually."

"Wow," I say. "So he's a cowboy and a builder. He's just one of those all-round handy guys."

"He's quite useful to have around at times," Annie admits.

"To fix a leaky tap," I say with a grin, "or hang a picture."

"Exactly. And I usually can get him to do it for free."

We laugh as we stride down the main street. The people we pass stop to say hello to Annie and ask her how her parents are doing, wishing her happy Christmas.

Next we enter the craft shop, and the little old lady running the store seems to know Annie too.

"I've always wanted to learn how to crochet," I mutter as we browse the shelves.

"Excellent," Annie says. "Then you should learn."

She takes my hand and takes me back to the counter

where the little old lady with curly white hair and a pair of spectacles hanging around her neck on a chain is reading a magazine.

"Priscilla," Annie says, "this is my friend Hollie. She wants to learn to crochet."

Priscilla lifts her spectacles onto her nose and examines me through them. "An excellent hobby," she says. "What crafting skills do you possess?"

"Absolutely none," I tell her.

"So a beginner." She steps out from behind the counter and hobbles to a shelf full of needles and balls of wool. Humming to herself, she picks a few things out and hands them to me along with a book.

"There are lots of videos on the YouTube," she says. "Or – that's what they tell me. But this book is a good place to start as well. Everything you need to know about crocheting."

"Ah, okay," I say. I'd only mentioned it, but now it seems I am going to have a new hobby.

"We'll take it," Annie announces, then whispers into my ear as Priscilla rings it up, "You can make me one of those cute little crochet dicks."

"It'll be my first project," I tell her.

And maybe I'll make a decoration for Mrs. J to hang on her tree and a pair of oven gloves for Mr. J.

My heart is light and happy and bursting and when we step out of the store, it's snowing again.

I think I freaking love this place.

Chapter Twelve

H ollie

My best friend looks up at the sky and frowns. "I was gonna take you for hot chocolate and muffins at the diner," she tells me, "but this looks like it could be heavy snow and Dina's not a fan of that."

"Dina?" I say.

"My truck.".

I glance down the street to where the rust bucket is parked. "Is Dina going to make it back to the ranch, Annie? We're not going to get stuck in a snowdrift, are we?"

Annie snorts. "This is not some kind of Christmas movie, Hollie. And anyway, the snow's light now, it's just a precaution."

Except Dina obviously disagrees, because when Annie turns the ignition several minutes later, the engine does nothing. Not a rumble, not a cough, not a splutter. It's deadly silent. Annie's not perturbed. After all, it took three attempts to start the truck last time. She turns the key a second time. A second time, nothing happens. The third time is exactly the same, and the fourth, and the fifth, and the sixth. By the tenth time, Annie finally admits defeat.

"Darn it," she says. "You can't die on me right before Christmas, Dina."

As soon as she says the words, she realizes what she's said, glancing my way in horror. "I'm so sorry, Hollie."

"Don't worry about it, Annie. You don't have to refrain from mentioning death in front of me for evermore. It won't actually kill me."

"I know," she says. "I just don't want to make you sad."

"Make me sad? I've just had the most amazing morning and I'm going to spend my afternoon crocheting mini dicks." I grin at her. "That's if we can make it back to the house."

"Yeah," Annie tugs out her cell phone and hits dial, "I'll call Dad," she says, bringing the cell up to her ear. Annie explains to her dad what's happened. Then she hangs up and turns to me. "Looks like it's hot chocolate and muffins in the diner after all."

We jump back down from the truck and trudge our way through the snow to the diner. It's toasty warm inside, and I'm more than happy to while away more time drinking coffee, eating muffins, and having Annie point out the other regulars in the diner, who they are, and little stories about each one of them.

"I can't believe you know everyone in this town," I say in disbelief.

"Well, there's only 3,000 of us," Annie says. "There's not that many to know."

"Doesn't it get ... you know, claustrophobic at times? Everyone knowing your business and all that stuff."

"Nope," Annie says, "because it's kind of nice. And people always help each other out in this town. Like when Dad's knee finally gave up the ghost – there was a week while Mom was sick with the flu in bed – and the neighbors delivered them home-cooked food every night, and after Clay's accident and he needed specialist back surgery in New York, the community rallied round to raise the funds for him to go."

"What?" I say, halting mid-muffin-bite. "What accident?"

My friend glares at me like she can't believe I don't know what she's talking about. But I don't. I have no idea.

"The accident he had when he was eighteen. You know, the one that ended his big rodeo dreams."

I shake my head. "You never told me about that."

Annie grimaces. "I didn't? I guess it's something none of us likes to talk about. Bad memories," she visibly shudders. "I saw it happen. For a moment, I thought ... well, I thought he was dead."

"Shit! What *did* happen?"

"He got thrown from a horse in a rodeo competition. Which was nothing new for Clay. He knows how to fall from a horse and not get hurt." I shudder – I can't imagine ever falling from a horse and not being hurt by it. "But that one time he landed in this crazy-ass position and it broke his back. He's lucky he's still walking."

"I had no idea."

"Like I said, it's not something we talk about." She scoops cream from the top of her hot chocolate and licks it off the spoon. "Anyway, the only downside of living in a small town like Silver Creek," Annie says, "and the reason I moved away in the first place, is the serious lack of men."

I wonder if that's strictly true – after all, there's three eligible, available Alphas back at Big Sky Ranch, and Annie herself seems to have found herself one hot barman. "So what's going to happen when the Christmas break ends?" I ask her, thinking of said hot barman. "You're going back to Lamford and you're leaving Travis behind?"

"I'm not sure," she says. "At first I thought it was just a festive fling, but I really like him." She turns her cell phone on the table, hits a button, and her screen fills with messages, all from Travis, the barman.

"He's really keen," I say.

"I'm really keen. I think we might try the long-distance thing. Or maybe..."

"Maybe?" I say.

"I was thinking of moving back," she tells me.

"Really?"

I've always known that Annie loved her home, but I also thought she had bigger ideas and bigger ambitions. Once she moved away, I thought that would be it for her. Seems I was wrong.

"Yeah," she continues, "and not just because of Travis. I miss this place, I miss this town, I miss the fresh air, the countryside, I miss the horses, I miss my mom and dad. Sometimes," she says, "I even miss Clay," she rolls her eyes, "although those times are few and far between."

"You really do hate your big brother, don't you?" I tease.

"No," she says. "I don't hate him."

I raise an eyebrow at her.

"Seriously, Hollie. He annoys the heck out of me. But that's all big brothers, isn't it? He's a good guy, really. He'd make a really good partner for an Omega one day," she says, giving me a look.

"You're not insinuating ..."

"I saw the way you looked at him when he was cutting down that tree yesterday."

"Any woman would have looked at him that way."

"You're a pervert, Hollie Bright," she tells me.

"You're the one requesting I crochet you mini dicks," I remind her.

"True." She tips back her mug and finishes the last of her hot chocolate, a big dollop of cream ending up on the end of her nose. I decide I'm not going to tell her about it.

She spins her cell phone back toward herself and peers at the time. "Do you want another one?" she says, pointing at our mugs. "Dad should be here any minute, but we could probably convince him to join us."

I peer out at the window where it's now snowing heavily, lovely big clumps of white dust falling from the gray clouds that hang in the sky above the town. A few trucks and vehicles rumble along the main street, their headlights shining, their wipers swishing. I'm on the lookout for Mr. J. Instead, I spy Clay Jackson in his truck. I expect him to drive right by us. Instead, he swings his truck into a space and then he's hopping out, knocking his hat onto his head as he does.

"Talking of the devil," I say, pointing her brother out to Annie.

"Oh," Annie moans. "I bet Mom's sent him to get us instead of Dad."

"You just said–"

"I know, I know. But I'm going to get a lecture," she tells me.

Clay spots us through the window, waves, and his little

sister beckons him inside. He hesitates for a moment, his gaze finding mine, and then he's pushing on the diner door and striding inside. There's something about the man – his large frame, his good looks, his confident swagger – that has everybody in the diner turning to glance his way.

"Howdy," he mutters, tipping his hat at everyone, and then joining us at the table. "You ready to go, ladies?" he asks.

"Actually," Annie says, "we were going to have another of these." She motions at the hot chocolate. "Maybe you'd like to join us?" He looks a little surprised at that suggestion. "It's Christmas, after all," Annie reminds him.

"Okay," he grunts.

"Great," Annie says. "You can grab them for us."

He glares at her. "I walked right into that one, didn't I?"

"Yep," Annie says.

And I giggle at the two of them. I always wished I'd had a sibling, and as much as Annie does moan about her brother and as much as he rolls his eyes at his little sister, I can see how much they care about each other. Mom's illness and everything that happened afterwards would have been a whole lot easier to handle if there'd have been someone to share that burden with.

"How do you take your hot chocolate, Hollie?" he asks me.

"Cream, a chocolate flake, marshmallows – the works," I tell him.

He snorts. "I suppose you take your coffee the same way."

"Nope. I like my coffee blacker than the depths of hell."

He raises an eyebrow at that.

"That's also how Clay likes his coffee," Annie says, "because it suits his mood and his soul."

Clay scowls at his little sister. "Be careful, or I'll be coming back with just a water for you."

"You wouldn't dare."

He smirks and marches toward the counter.

"He better not come back with water," she mutters.

But he doesn't. He returns a moment later with our two hot chocolates – cream, marshmallows, flakes and all – and for him, just that black coffee. He also has a plate of something balanced in his hands. He deposits it all on the table and takes the seat opposite me and Annie.

"What's that?" I ask him, pointing to the rich-looking tart in front of him.

"This, Hollie Bright, is wild berry tart. Ever tried it before?"

I shake my head.

"Then you need to try it now. You can't come visit the Rockies, you can't come visit Silver creek, and not try some." He slides the plate over to me and passes me the fork, our fingertips brushing together ever so briefly, but it's enough to send electricity scooting up my arm. "It's cooked with berries picked from the county, and Eileen makes the best pie this side of Denver."

I nod with approval and sink the prongs of my fork into the gooey-looking tart. I scoop it up along with a bit of cream and place it inside my mouth. The taste is immediately sweet and surprisingly tangy, and I groan with satisfaction.

"Oh my goodness, that's good," I say, passing the fork back to him.

He shakes his head. "I got it for you."

"Clay doesn't eat sweet things," Annie says.

And I swear the Alpha's eyes flash at those words, something his sister doesn't spot, but I definitely do.

"I can't eat all this," I say. "I already ate pancakes for breakfast, and we had a chocolate chip muffin before you arrived. You have to share it with me."

"Told you," Annie says. "Clay doesn't eat sweet things."

I ignore my best friend, scoop up another piece of pie, and offer it up to the Alpha sitting across from me. He meets my gaze for a moment and then he's leaning forward, opening his mouth, and I swear my arm starts shaking as I feed him the piece of pie between his lips. He captures the prongs of the fork between his lips for just a second, holding my gaze in his, and then he slides them along the prong, releasing them, chewing, swallowing, and licking his lips.

"Surprised he didn't spit it out," Annie mutters.

And I jolt. For a moment I'd forgotten she was there.

"Can I have some?" Annie asks.

"Oh, yeah, sure," I say.

Annie snatches the fork from my hand and slides the plate toward her.

"It's really good," I say. "I'm going to have to get the recipe."

Clay says nothing. He's still staring at me. And because that's really intense, I start blabbing in the way I always do when a handsome man captures me in his gaze. Not that that's ever happened before.

"My mom used to make apple pie. She got the recipe from her mom, who got it from her mom, who got it from her mom. And she taught me how to make it. It's possibly the best apple pie ever," I say.

"I'd like to try that," Clay says.

Annie almost chokes on her mouthful. "What's happened to you, Clay Jackson?" she says.

"Nothing." He picks up his mug and takes a long swig

of coffee as he sits back in his chair. "I've always liked apple pie."

Annie offers me up the last remaining piece of the wild berry pie, and I gobble it up, finishing my hot chocolate, trying not to notice the way the Alpha is still staring at me. When I'm finished, I have to admit I feel just a little bit queasy.

"I need to eat a ton of carrots now," I say, "and lettuce. I actually feel quite sick."

"You're not going to vomit on me again, are you?" Clay asks – although he says it with just a hint of a smile that makes me think ... is he flirting with me?

"You better sit in the front seat, then," Annie says, wiping her mouth on the napkin. "Otherwise, Clay's driving is likely to make you vomit."

"I drive a hell of a lot better than you do, Annie. And I've never run my truck into the ground."

"Your truck is like a year old," Annie says. "Mine is over 20."

"Yeah, and not moving anywhere today, is it?" he says, thumbing in the direction of the two trucks parked out front. "Anyway, better get going." He peers over his shoulder. "Snow's getting heavier."

Chapter Thirteen

C lay

There's something about having Hollie Bright riding beside me in my truck that's sending all of my Alpha instincts into somersaults, or maybe that's just her scent, thick and rich and sweet as hell this afternoon. She also looks incredibly cute, all wrapped up in her thick winter coat. Cheeks rosy from the cold. Eyes wide as she watches the heavy snow falling all around us.

"How can you see?" she asks me for possibly the tenth time.

I want to remind her that Alphas have good eyesight, that our senses are heightened when there's an Omega in our presence, especially an Omega we have a desire to protect, but my little sister's sitting in the back of the cab, eyes boring into the back of my neck. So I just tell her,

"Well practiced, done this hundreds and hundreds of times. Trust me."

"Oh, I trust you," she blurts out. I turn my head to glance at her "I just wouldn't want to do it myself."

I force my gaze back to the windshield, which is becoming increasingly more difficult because all I want to do is sit and watch this girl. She's mesmerizing, entrancing. So darn beautiful.

I have a desire to tell her all that. I think I must be high on the sugar from the wild berry pie. Or maybe that's just her scent. Yet again.

Shit, I need to get my head together. Stop acting like a damn fool. I grip the steering wheel more tightly as if to steady myself.

"Can't we have some music or something?" my sister says from the back of the cab. "I know you hate music, and fun in general, but it is Christmas."

"He needs to concentrate," Hollie says, sticking up for me and taking my side for once, sending a strange sensation fluttering in my chest.

"Would you like some music, Hollie?" I ask her, making my sister huff and flop back on her seat, arms crossed grumpily across her chest.

"Shall I see what I can find?" She turns the knob on my radio. It crackles and murmurs, the snow impacting the reception. But finally she finds a station, and it's playing the usual Christmas jingles.

"I love this one," Hollie says, smiling brightly now and sending more of those crazy sensations tumbling in my body.

She hums along to the tune and it takes all the willpower I have not to skid us off the road, to cut the engine and to pull the woman into my lap. The drive takes forever, and that is nothing to do with the conditions of the road. It's torturous. How the hell am I meant to get through the next few days? I knew it would be tough. I figured that much out after we picked her up at the airport. But it's definitely getting tougher. I'm going to have to find excuses to avoid the house. I'm going to have to find work that needs doing on the far side of our land. I need to stay out of this woman's path.

A few moments later, we see the beams of another truck coming toward us in the opposite direction and then my little sister is jumping forward in her seat again and tapping me on the shoulder.

"That's Travis' truck," she says, "Blink your lights."

I mutter under my breath as she punches my arm.

"I'm not sure I like Travis."

"He's a million times nicer than any other dude I've dated. Don't you agree, Hollie?"

Hollie has spoken barely a handful of words to the bartender from the *Dirty Boot*, but she always has her best friend's back and nods. "He seems really nice."

"Fine," I say, flicking the lights on and off, on and off, then slowing the truck down as Travis does the same until we're parking up alongside each other. I wind my window down and Travis does the same with his.

"Hey there, folks," he says, eyes flicking around the cab and sparking with excitement when he spots my little sister.

"Hey, man," I say.

"I was just swinging by your ranch," he says. "Dropping by to say hello. I got a Christmas present for you too, Annie."

I resist the urge to snort a second time. The ranch is a good 20 minutes outside of town and in the opposite direction from where Travis lives. But he's certainly got a thing for my sister, and she's right, he's not so bad. For starters, he has a job, a house, and a truck. It's a lot more than that of the other idiots my little sister has dated.

"I've got a present for you too," Annie says, leaning over my shoulder to talk to Travis through the open window. "Back at the ranch, you've got time to come back there with us now?"

"Sure," Travis says, smile broadening across his face.

"Great," Annie responds.

And before I know it, she's jumping out of my truck, running around Travis's in the snow and jumping in his passenger door. She waves at us through the window. "We'll see you back at the ranch," she says. I go to argue, but Travis's window is zipping up and his truck is rumbling away.

"I thought girl code stipulates that you aren't meant to ditch your best friend for a dude," I mutter to Hollie, outraged on her behalf and starting the engine a little too aggressively, nearly sliding on the snow as I jerk the machine forward.

Hollie simply shrugs. "She's completely loved up. You can't blame her. And people do crazy things when they're in love."

I swing my gaze back to the windshield. Blood hums in my ears. It suddenly feels crazy warm in the cab.

"Have you ever been in love?" I ask her, because I'm an idiot and I can't help myself.

She's quiet for a moment and then she says, "No, I don't think I have been. I mean, once or twice I thought I was, but now, looking back, it wasn't the real thing. But I'm hopeful, you know, that it's out there for me too."

She's quiet for another moment and then she says,

"How about you, Clay Jackson? Have you ever been in love before?"

I shake my head. "No, same as you really. There were one or two girls, but it wasn't real. I wouldn't have moved mountains for them."

"That's the test?" she says, and I can hear the smile in her voice. "You have to want to move mountains for someone to be in love?"

"Absolutely," I say. "I think they have to be someone you want to spend all your time with, that you never want to be apart from, that you'd do anything for."

"Yeah," she says. "I think you're right. I think that's what love is."

I glance her way. She's not looking at me anymore. She's looking out through the windshield, gaze glazed over. She's thinking. I hope I haven't made her sad again. Because I want her to be happy. And I wonder, is that another sign that you're in love with someone and if so does that mean I'm in love with Hollie Bright?

The realization nearly has me skidding off the road. In love with Hollie Bright?! That can't be right. That can't be happening.

"How did you meet your packmates?" Hollie asks me, pulling me out of the mini crisis happening inside my head.

I scratch at the back of my neck. "Tucker and I go way back–"

"All the way to kindergarten," Hollie interjects.

"Yeah," I say. "Yeah, that's right."

"Nash isn't from round here though, is he?" Hollie says.

"No. But he had a job on another of the ranches in the area. Wasn't really working out, so I offered him a job on our ranch."

"And how did you decide to become a pack? How did

you know you wanted to be together for the rest of your lives?"

"I guess we just bonded."

"You did?"

"You may have noticed," I shuffle on my seat, "that sometimes I can be a little ill-tempered. Tucker, he's not like that – he's always in a good mood. And I'm not always as sensitive as I could be. And Nash. Well he is. It brings a sort of balance to the pack."

"Not sunshiny and not sensitive," Hollie says. And I swear I hear that smile in her voice again. "Are you saying, Clay Jackson, that you're a grump?"

"Tucker says I'm a Grinch."

Hollie laughs. "And do you agree?"

"Probably," I say sulkily, "it's just the way I am."

"Hmm," Hollie says, and this time I can't help flicking my gaze once again toward her. She's sitting back in the seat of my truck, looking mighty comfortable, and I wouldn't mind it if she spent the rest of my days riding alongside me like this.

"There are certain things," I tell her, "that make me less grumpy, less grouchy, though." *You, for starters,* I think in my head.

"Like what?"

"The ranch, the cattle, the horses, my family, my pack."

"Yeah. I can see how that would be. I feel a whole weight lifting off my shoulders just being in this place. It's been a little lonely back in Rockview lately."

We turn off the main road onto the track. It's stupid, but I don't want this ride to end. I want to have this moment with her, just the two of us, and I want it to stretch on for as long as it can.

"You shouldn't be alone," I tell her. More words blurting out of my mouth without my consent.

"No, I guess no one should," she says. "In some ways, I think you Alphas are lucky, having packs and everything."

"An Omega can have a pack," I say. And there's a little bit of a growl in my voice which I try to disguise with a cough.

I don't know if she notices but she says next, "I never thought that's what I wanted."

There's a pause. A tension in the air, words unsaid.

"Do you think?" I ask. "Do you think you might be changing your mind?"

I pull up outside the house, cut the engine, turn in the seat to look at her. Her checks are bright red. She's staring out the window.

"I don't know," she whispers.

"Hollie," I say. And her eyes snatch my way. As soon as our gazes collide, it's like fireworks explode in my blood. I want this woman. I want her so badly. Not just in this moment, but probably forever more.

So I do the only thing I can do. I unbuckle my belt. I unbuckle her belt. I lean across the space between us and I kiss Hollie Bright.

I don't know if I half expect her to pull away, to push me away, to jump out of my truck and run as fast as she can away from me. But she does none of those things. Instead, she kisses me right back, her soft lips moving against mine. She tastes of sweet wild berry pie and her mouth is soft and warm.

It's been a while since I kissed a girl. It's been even longer since I've wanted to kiss a girl this badly, but I don't think a kiss has ever been quite like this one, has had all these sensations somersaulting in my stomach, has had my skin skating with electricity, has had my scent spiraling in the air.

I reach across the space, sliding my hand into her hair and pressing her mouth more firmly against mine, parting her lips with my tongue and sinking inside her warm mouth. She makes a little moaning sound that has me stiffening in my pants. And I'm about to do what I've wanted to do this whole entire ride home – pull her right into my lap – but then I hear the sound of tires crunching on snow and I snap away from her.

Chapter Fourteen

H ollie

I sit in the seat of Clay Jackson's truck, dazed and confused, blinking like mad, my skin tingling, because did that just really happen? Did Clay Jackson just kiss me? Kissed me like I've never been kissed before. Kissed me in a way that has me severely tempted to crawl straight across the gap between us and straddle his lap.

I'm speechless, which means we're both sitting in his truck in silence, listening to the truck behind us cut its engine and the cab doors open and shut. Footsteps crunch across the snow and it's then that Clay finally decides to speak.

"Hollie, I–"

But he doesn't get any further because the truck door swings open and Annie's tugging on my arm.

"What the hell are you two doing just sitting in the truck?"

We both glance at each other and I'm sure I have "guilty" written right across my forehead in marker pen. Then we glance back at Clay's sister.

"Waiting for you," Clay says.

"Oh–kay," Annie answers. "Well, I'm here now, so are you going to keep on just sitting in the truck? Or are we going inside?"

"I've got to get back to the cabin," Clay mutters.

"Will we see you later?" I say as light and breezily as I can, because I have a hell of a lot of emotions running riot through my body right now.

"I don't know," he says.

And I don't know how to take that response. *He* kissed *me*. Does he already regret it? Was it a mistake?

My belt's already unbuckled on account of the fact that Clay Jackson unbuckled it for me so that he could kiss me properly, so I slide out of my seat and jump down onto the snow. It's really blizzarding out here now. I can barely see the house, which is only a few feet away from us. Annie slams the truck door shut and we walk with Travis to the house as Clay drives his truck away.

"Is it me?" Annie says. "Or is that brother of mine acting even more weird than usual?"

"I think weirdness must run in the family," I say, which makes Travis chuckle.

"Hey," Annie says to him, "if you want that Christmas present, just remember whose side you're on."

"Your side, sweetheart," he says, in a way that clearly has Annie charmed.

When we reach the door, I can't help glancing over my

shoulder, watching as Clay's truck rumbles along the track. The pack's cabin is probably the only place on the ranch I haven't seen yet. Annie told me it sits a mile from the main house on the other side of the creek. I'm not even sure where that is, but now I can't help imagining it. Does it have a nest for an Omega?

I have my own nest back in Rockview, one I've built on the side of my bedroom for my heats – heats I've always spent alone unless I've had a beta boyfriend at the time who's been willing to help me out. Although, most find the whole thing gross. That's what they say, anyway. I've always wondered if their aversion to it has actually been because they feel inadequate. They're not Alphas after all. They have no knot. They're never going to fall into a rut. They're never going to be able to fuck me for three days straight.

I shake my head. I really do not need to be thinking of nests, heats and ruts right now. If I let those thoughts creep into my head, I'll start slicking and that will be game over. Although, you can hardly blame a girl. That one kiss, a kiss which probably barely lasted a minute, was enough to have my whole body melting. Another minute and I would most definitely have been slicking and things in that truck would have got a hell of a lot more steamy.

Once we're in the house, Annie says to me, "I'm gonna show Travis the tree and then we're gonna swap Christmas presents."

"Is that what the kids are calling it these days?"

Annie gives me an unimpressed scowl. "My parents are in the room next door. Anyway, do you want to join us?" Before I can turn that suggestion into something lewd, she adds, "for present exchange."

I lift my shopping bag. "No, I think I'm going to make a start on that crochet project."

"You sure?" she said. "You're gonna be okay?"

"Annie," I say. "I'm perfectly fine."

I think my best friend forgets I spent the last few months alone in Rockview. Okay, she's been checking up on me as often as she can, sending me text messages and video calling me. But I spent a lot of time on my own, thinking, grieving, trying to get my life together. Most of my time I've spent working because, like I told Mrs. J, animals are the one thing that truly lift my spirits right now.

"As long as you're sure," Annie says.

I nod and head up to my bedroom where I spread out all my new crocheting equipment on the bed and start searching the internet for crocheting instruction videos, except before I know it, I'm searching for videos of men swinging axes and chopping wood instead, because I can't get that image out of my mind, and I can't get that chocolate fudge scent of Clay's out of my nose either, and I definitely can't get the feel of his lips on mine and his hand in my hair from my memory either.

I flop back on the bed.

I'm in trouble, real trouble.

Am I catching feelings for Clay Jackson? Am I catching feelings for his pack mates too? Or maybe this is just a severe case of the hornies. After all, it's been a long time since I got laid. Perhaps, a little light relief is all I need. Take the edge off all these hormones racing around my body and then I'll be back on an even keel and the three hot Alphas striding around this ranch will have no effect on me at all.

I make sure I've locked the bedroom door after myself and then I switch off my phone. I don't need any of those videos. I have one I can play in my own head. I slide my hand into my panties and touch myself and then, with that image of Clay Jackson swinging his axe, and the memory of his lips pressed against mine, I make myself come.

Chapter Fifteen

Tucker

I'm washing up in the bathroom when I hear the cabin door slam open and shut and footsteps stomp across the floor. I recognize them immediately – Clay – and by the volume of those stomps I can tell that something's clearly wrong.

I sling a clean T-shirt over my head and go out to investigate, finding him pacing in the kitchen.

"What's up, man?" I say, heading to the fridge to hook out two bottles of beer. I snap off the lids and pass one to him.

He's still pacing, and he ignores the outstretched beer.

"Damn it!" he mutters. "Damn, damn, damn."

Now I'm concerned. I take a step backwards in alarm. "What the fuck, Clay? What the fuck is wrong? Is it the cattle? Is it one of the horses?"

"I kissed Hollie Bright," he says, not pausing in his pacing.

It takes several seconds for those words to compute. That was not what I was expecting him to say, nor does it account for this stress-head behavior.

"You kissed the Omega?" I say, flopping down into the nearest chair and taking a swig of my beer. "I'm taking it she didn't approve of that action? Did you get a slap around the face? A berating from Annie?"

"Me? No. No, actually, she..." He stops pacing and rubs his hand over his face. "She kissed me back."

"In a felt-obliged-to-do-so manner, or in a sucking-your-soul-from-your-body kind of manner?"

"It wasn't long enough for any soul-sucking," he says, "but it was definitely more toward that end."

"Wow! Clay, man, this is great news!"

He drops his hand away from his face and looks at me aghast. "No, it's not. This is the worst."

I can't help chuckling. "How is this the worst? You kissed a girl you like. The girl obviously likes you back because she kissed you too."

"I don't like her," he snaps automatically.

"Oh, come on, man," I say. "You're crazy about her. It's written all over your face. And I know your scent well, Clay Jackson. I've known you since the second day of kindergarten. I know when you like a girl. I can read it in your scent."

"Fine," he snaps. "I like her. Doesn't mean she likes me back. And also, if you've happened to forget, she's Annie's best friend."

"So what?" I say.

"My parents really care about her."

"That's a good thing, Clay. Imagine if they hated her."

"I can't afford to fuck things up."

"Who says you're going to fuck things up?"

He gives me a look. "I always fuck things up, especially when it comes to women."

"That's because they weren't the right kind of women," I tell him. "Hollie Bright, gee, she seems like the right kind of woman to me."

"You like her too?" he asks.

"You know I do, Clay. I really like her. And Nash does too."

He takes the spare beer from my hand, presses it to his lips, and knocks back at least half of it in one long gulp.

"I don't know what to do," he says when he tips his head back and wipes his hand across his mouth.

"What would you like to do?" I ask, feeling a lot like Clay Jackson's therapist right now.

"I'd like to kiss her again," he says.

I chuckle. "I'd like to do a whole lot more than just kissing with that girl."

"She said," he looks at the floor and then back up at me, "that she's changing her mind about packs. That she never thought she wanted one, but now..."

"She said that?" I say, almost jumping up from my seat. "She wants a pack? Do you think she meant our pack?"

"I doubt it," he mutters.

"Oh, come on," I say. "She's had a rethink about the situation since she's known us. That's got to be down to our influence. This could be our chance, Clay."

"It could also land us in a whole heap of trouble."

I can tell my friend is not going to be easily convinced by this. To be honest, he's rarely convinced by anything. He's the negative to my positive, the pessimism to my optimism. It wasn't always that way. My best friend used to have a much sunnier outlook on life. But it's one of the reasons our friendship works as well as it does, why it's lasted all this time. We need each other to balance each other out.

"I'd be happy to find myself in a whole heap of trouble with Hollie Bright," I say with a grin, imagining what that would look like. "Does she taste like she smells, Clay?"

"Better," he says. "She tastes a whole lot better."

I whistle. "I can only imagine what she tastes like between her legs, Clay. Imagine that."

"That's all I've been imagining," he says. "Damn."

"Don't be so hard on yourself," I tell him. "We're Alphas. We're programmed for this. Of course, throwing an Omega into our midst was gonna drive us kind of crazy. Especially an Omega like her."

"I just..." He looks down into his beer bottle and swirls the liquid around. "I don't want to hurt her, Tucker. The girl's been through a lot. I can see it, can't you, in her eyes?"

I nod. "It's hard to lose anyone, Clay. Especially a mom. Especially when it was just the two of them." He's silent. I don't have to tell him how well I understand Hollie's situation. We'd already been the best of friends for well over a decade when I lost my mom, when I lost my dad for all shapes and purposes too, and ended up practically living at Big Sky Ranch. "We won't hurt her, Clay. We're not those kinds of men. We're not like that."

"I know. But sometimes these things happen without you meaning them to. And I don't want to be that guy."

"You know what I say? I think we should stop imagining what the Omega does and doesn't want. I think we should stop making that decision for her, and I think we should ask her. I feel this could be it for us, Clay."

My best friend lifts his gaze to mine. "I don't know," he says. "Life doesn't seem to work out the way you want it to."

I cock my head to one side. Is he talking about the accident? He never talks about the accident. He hasn't talked about it for as long as I can remember.

"No it doesn't," I say softly. "But that doesn't mean every other thing in your life isn't going to go the way you want it to either. And things haven't worked out so bad, have they?"

"No ... it's just sometimes I feel like I was robbed of my future, my chance, or something."

"Clay," I say, "I've never said this to you before, because you're my best friend, man, and I love you to bits. But I don't think you'd have lasted on the rodeo circuit. I think you'd've been home within six months."

"What?" he gasps, gaze flying to meet mine. "How could you say that, Tucker?"

"Because it's true. I know you. I sometimes think I know you better than you know yourself. You would have been home sick. You would have been lonely. You were made to be a rancher like your dad – not some big rodeo hotshot star." He stares at me sulkily. I don't blame him. The truth can be hard to hear. "Know what else I know?"

"No. But I have a feeling you're going to tell me."

"That girl was made for you. She was made for us."

Chapter Sixteen

Nash

I'm grooming the horses at the end of the day when I catch a whiff of that honey scent.

Hollie.

"Hey," she says, walking into the barn. "Mrs. J said you were out here seeing to the horses, and I thought I'd come give you a hand, if that's okay."

"Always appreciate any offer of help," I tell her.

She smiles and goes to fetch a set of brushes, returning into the store and helping me with Bonnie.

"I don't think I could ever get tired of this," she says.

"No, me neither. I like it, especially at the end of the day. Kind of puts me at peace."

"It's mindful," Hollie says.

"Yes, that's it. Mindful," I say, nodding my head.

"Is the job hard then – running a ranch?" she asks. "Is it stressful?"

"No. It's freaking hard work, but most of the time it's enjoyable. Obviously there are times when it's tough – when we lose a calf, when one of the horses is injured – but the good times definitely outnumber the bad. And sometimes you have to go down through the lows to appreciate the highs."

"I think you're right," Hollie says, dragging the brush over Bonnie's rump and then stroking her hand over the smooth fur in a way that has me captivated. "Annie says you're gonna be building a house."

"Yeah. As soon as the spring comes, when the frost breaks and the snow melts. As soon as the ground is soft enough, we're going to start."

"Whereabouts are you going to build it?" she asks me.

"Next to our cabin. It's the perfect spot. Best views of the mountains from there."

"It sounds amazing," she says.

And then I hear her shuffle on her feet. She wants to say something, but she's nervous, and this causes me to look up at her face.

"Annie says you're going to start a family."

"In an ideal world," I say, watching her expression. "Of course, we have to find the right woman first."

She's not meeting my eye.

"Oh," she says breezily. "There isn't a special girl at the moment then?"

"No." I stop what I'm doing. I wait for her to flick her gaze to mine. "But I think there could be."

"Clay kissed me," she blurts out, which is not what I expected her to say.

My gaze automatically falls to her lips. Pink, plush, soft-looking.

"I don't blame him. I'd love to kiss you too, Hollie."

"You would?" she squeaks, her honey scent spiraling in the air – so sweet, so delicious.

"Very much so," I tell her. "If you'd let me."

"I'd let you," she whispers, her pupils darkening.

I want to kiss her now, but there's a horse between us. I walk round to the front of Bonnie, duck under her neck, and come to stand in front of Hollie. She peers up, her head tipping right back.

"Can I kiss you now?" I ask her.

"Will Clay mind?" she says a little shyly. "I'm sorry, I don't know how it works with packs."

"In packs we share. We share everything. Clay won't mind me kissing you, Hollie, as long as it's what you want."

"It's what I want," she whispers.

I reach out and take a hold of her fingers in my hand, and for a moment I just stroke my thumb over her knuckles. Even just that simple gesture has everything in my body tingling, and I think it has the same effect on her too.

I take a step toward her, pulling her toward me as I do. She comes willingly into my arms and I wrap them around her waist.

"I've wanted to kiss you from the moment I met you, Hollie Bright," I tell her.

"Because you're a hopeless romantic and fall in love with every woman you meet," she says, with a hint of a smile. She's teasing me.

"No," I say, deadly serious. "Because you're the most amazing woman I've ever met."

And then I lean down and I kiss her. And God, the woman tastes so sweet, I get a rush to the head. I groan, pulling her right up against me, feeling how soft and supple her body is against mine.

I kiss her like a girl ought to be kissed – deep, passionate, slow.

And she kisses me back, sighing into my mouth with such sweetness it has my knees almost buckling.

She reaches up, entwines her arms around my neck, and drags me down, kissing me with even more urgency. Beside us, the horse huffs and stomps her hooves, but we both ignore her, too wrapped up in each other.

I usually pride myself on being a gentleman, but Hollie Bright does things to me I can't explain. I can't help myself. I slide my hands from her waist and take a grip of her fine ass, squeezing it between my palms. She gives a little whimper, and the next thing I know, I'm walking her backwards until she hits the stable wall, and I'm grinding into her as I kiss her needy mouth, my tongue brushing up against hers.

And to my immense satisfaction, she grinds right back against me, whimpering this time, and the scent of something sweet permeating the air.

Slick. Is that slick?

Fuck. I'm making her slick.

"Hollie," I groan into her mouth, and then I'm kissing along her jaw to the shell of her ear. I swirl my tongue around it, whispering her name again, and then I'm sucking on her neck, sucking as I grind into her, lifting her leg and wrapping it around my waist so that I can grind right into where she needs me the most, where I bet she's throbbing.

"Oh God!" she mutters as I slide her sweater down her shoulder, my mouth following along, kissing the skin there and then lower, over her collarbone and her ribcage to the swell of her breasts.

"You smell so sweet, Omega," I tell her. "And you taste

even sweeter. I bet you taste, frankly, obscene between your legs."

"Oh my goodness," she squeals. "Where did you learn to speak like that? Not in any Jane Austen book."

"Just saying what I feel," I say, running my hands up her ass, her hips, squeezing her waist. Fuck, she feels so good – all of her.

Her hands are in my hair, and she's scraping her nails against my scalp. The action sends me kind of feral.

I kiss her again, grinding into her more powerfully, seeing how it makes her legs shake.

She's so sensitive – every little touch, every brush of my lips has her moaning, whimpering, shivering in my arms. I wonder how long it's been since she's been touched, since she's been kissed, since she's been pleasured. And oh fuck, this woman deserves to be pleasured. I want to pleasure her over and over and over again.

I bring my mouth back to her ear.

"Clay says you're not a fan of Alphas, Hollie."

"I could be changing my mind," she sighs. "I think I could be a very big fan."

"Have you .... Have you ever been with an Alpha before?"

She hesitates. "No. No, I haven't."

I groan like I've just been gutted. "You've never had a knot?"

The word has the girl shaking so violently in my arms, it takes all my willpower not to knot her here and now.

"N-no-no," she says. "I've never been ... I've never been knotted."

What a fucking waste. A pussy like her deserves to be knotted. "Would you like to be?" I say.

"Oh fuck, yes," she mutters.

I'm about to offer to take her home to our cabin right now and knot her all through the night, but the stable door flings open and Annie's calling for her best friend.

"Hollie! Hollie, where are you?"

It takes all my strength to drop the Omega back down on her feet and take a decisive step away from her, although I'm unable to drag my eyes from the woman.

She takes a deep inhale and runs her hands over her hair, taming the fly-away strands. To me, it's damn obvious the girl was seconds away from an orgasm – especially with me grinding into her pussy like that – but maybe Annie won't notice what's going on.

"I'm in here!" Hollie calls.

Annie races down the barn aisle and joins us a moment later in the stall. I turn back toward the horse, picking up where I left off.

"I knew you'd be in here," Annie says. "You just can't stay away, can you?"

"Erm, no," I hear Hollie say, her voice a little strained.

"I was going to put a Christmas movie on. Can we start it now, or do you need more time?"

"Give me a minute," Hollie says.

"Sure," Annie responds. "Hey, Nash," she says as she heads back toward the door.

"Hey, Annie," I say, convinced she must hear all the testosterone that's careening through my blood clear as day in my voice, that it must be obvious I was making out with her best friend only seconds ago.

"Geez," Hollie says. I turn around and find her shaking her head and taking another of those deep breaths. "It's probably just as well she interrupted. I think I was ten seconds away from begging you to knot me in the stables," she giggles.

I suppress the very real urge to growl.

I was ten seconds away from knotting her against the wall of the stable. And that ... that is not me.

The girl deserves more respect. She deserves to be romanced and wooed and all the good things.

She also didn't come to the ranch to be harassed by a pack of alphas who can't keep it in their pants.

The girl only just lost her mom. She came here for space, for the fresh air, to clear her head. She doesn't need the distraction or the confusion of three alphas trying to wrangle her into bed.

And above all that, it's Christmas. A time that has all the emotions swirling. An especially difficult time without her mom here.

She's vulnerable. I knew that, and I still kissed her. I still pushed her. I feel like a class-A cad.

What was I thinking? Annie would skin me alive. Most probably, her mom and dad would help her out.

"I apologize, Hollie," I say. "That wasn't how we treat ladies around here."

"It wasn't?" she says, frowning in confusion. Or is that disappointment?

"Hollie, I'm sorry for my behavior."

"Oh no, don't say that. Please don't apologize," she says. "You didn't do anything wrong." She smiles at me. "In fact, you did a whole lot right. That's the problem."

I can't help smiling back at her. Fuck, I want to kiss her again. But if I kiss you again right now, I'm not sure I could control myself.

"I better go," she says, smiling again, and then, to my surprise, reaching out to squeeze my fingers. "I'll see you tomorrow. Christmas Eve."

"Christmas Eve," I say, hating myself all the more.

Chapter Seventeen

Clay

Nash arrives back at the cabin an hour after us, just as I'm about to serve up dinner. I'm not the world's greatest cook, but it's something that helps me take my mind off things. And right now, I'm trying really hard to take my mind off Hollie Bright and that kiss – especially after my conversation with Tucker.

My packmate thinks this is a good sign. He thinks we could have something with the girl. But I'm just not so sure. I don't think we're that lucky – I'm not sure I'm that lucky. And besides, a girl like Hollie Bright, she could have her pick of packs, she could have anyone she wanted. Why the hell would she choose us? Why the hell would a city girl like her want to become a pack omega out here in the mountains?

She wouldn't.

"Hey," Nash says as he walks into the cabin, tossing off his hat and toeing off his boots. He strides straight to the sink, rolling up his shirt sleeves and scrubbing his hands and his forearms.

He smells.

He smells a lot like honey.

I'm guessing Tucker smells it too, because he's also staring at our pack mate silently. Nash only realizes when he turns back around from the sink, blinking behind his glasses.

"Got something to tell us?" Tucker asks, hands on hips. "You kissed her, didn't you?"

He nods. "She told me that Clay kissed her," he says, motioning his head in my direction. "And then I couldn't help myself. I asked if I could kiss her too."

"And she let you?" Tucker says, a great big fuck-off grin spreading across his face – one that reads *told you so* as clearly as day.

Yeah, and maybe he's right. For once, Tucker could be right. There's a chance. A chance here.

"Yes, she let me. In fact..." He scratches his ear. "We did a little more than kissing."

"Fuck," Tucker says, his grin now so big I'm surprised it doesn't split his cheeks. "Care to share? A bit of..."

"Don't get so excited, Tucker," Nash says. "There was just a bit of grinding, a bit of squeezing."

"That sounds like heaven," Tucker says. "Because the girl has a body designed for sin."

"Trust me," Nash responds. "She does."

"And then what happened?"

Nash shakes his head, pulls out a chair from the dining table, and sits himself down. "Then Annie interrupted us."

"Goddamn Annie," I mutter under my breath.

"And I got a goddamn hold of myself," Nash says.

"Huh?"

"She just lost her mom," Nash explains. "She's vulnerable, and she knows she is. It's not the right time for a relationship."

And I feel my jaw drop and my optimism plummet. A moment ago, Tucker had almost convinced me – convinced me that maybe, just maybe, we could have Hollie Bright. That maybe we could have her forever.

But I was right all along. That was a stupid idea. Hollie Bright doesn't need us. Why would she?

"It doesn't have to be a relationship," Tucker says. "We could, you know, just have a bit of fun."

"That's worse," Nash says. "That's not what she needs."

"She said that?" Tucker asks.

"Not in so many words," Nash answers. "But you saw how she was the other day. She's still grieving. Fucking about with a bunch of assholes is the last thing she needs."

"Speak for yourself," Tucker says, "I'm no asshole."

I drop the meat pie on the table and pull out a chair myself, sitting down. Suddenly, I don't have an appetite anymore. I'm not hungry at all.

"That's what I said," I tell them both.

"Maybe we could–"

"No," I say, cutting off Tucker and his incessant optimism. "You're right, I care about her and I want what's best for her. It isn't the right time for her, Tucker. It's best we leave the Omega well alone."

I just wonder if any of us has the willpower to do that.

Chapter Eighteen

Hollie

Annie insists we spend our evening curled up in front of the TV watching Christmas movies and drinking Mr. J's homemade eggnog. Snuggled up with the Christmas tree twinkling beside me, I can't help reliving the two different kisses from today.

Honestly, what has my life become? Even in the brief "ho" phase I went through in college, I never kissed two different men on the same day.

But Nash said that wasn't a problem, and I can't help believing him. Packs work differently. Packs, like he said, share. And I think as an Omega I'm meant to find every single member of the pack just as attractive as the other – I'm meant to want them all. Which is just as well because I don't think I could choose between them.

Although, wanting these alphas is definitely not what I

should be thinking about right now. I should be watching the small, funny child outwit the two dumb burglars. I should focus on that. I should not be thinking about wood chopping, throwing hay bales, grooming horses, and kisses with hot alphas. I'm meant to be spending quality time with my best friend – who has given up time she could've been spending with her own hot man to be with me – not lost in horny fantasies.

It isn't much better when I climb into bed that night either. It's as if the two alphas have unleashed something inside me. Men, sex, relationships have been so far from my mind the last few months that even my usual roaring Omega hormones have been subdued. But now it's like they flicked a switch inside me. My skin feels tingly, my cheeks feel hot, and my mind is racing with dirty, dirty thoughts.

I'm severely tempted to repeat the actions of earlier in the day and take the edge off all this roaring horniness, but I'm not sure that worked last time. It may have even made the situation worse. So I lie in bed like a good little celibate nun and eventually I fall asleep.

Unfortunately, my mind decides to be naughty all of its own accord, and my dreams are full of hot, semi-naked alphas swinging axes and offering to knot me. I wake up even more hot and flustered than I did falling asleep.

If Annie notices that there's something up with me, she doesn't say anything. Instead, she announces at breakfast that morning, "Seeing as there's a break in the weather, I thought today was the perfect day for a horse ride."

I peer up from where I'm busy giving Dolly ear-scratches and nearly bounce up and down on my seat and clap my hands. She's right, the sunshine is pouring through the window today and, though I'm sure it's still just as cold outside, the skies are clear and the mountains sparkling in the distance. It is truly beautiful, and I can only imagine what this place must be like in summer with the ranch baking in sunshine every day and the wildflowers blooming in the pastures.

We saddle up Sugar and Cloud, and then, with Dolly trotting along beside us, we're out in the sunshine, riding across the pastures, over the creek, through the Christmas tree copse and out the other side. Then, before I know it, Annie's pointing to a large cabin nestled up on the slope.

"That's their cabin," she says. "Clay's and his pack."

I stare at it. It's much bigger than I'd imagined. Much sturdier-looking. In fact, it looks pretty luxurious from the outside, all clean pine wood and flashes of glass, and I realize that Nash is correct. It has the most incredible view out across the valley and the mountains, and I can imagine waking up to that every day would be simply amazing.

"You want to go say hi to the boys?" Annie asks me, and I scrutinize her face, looking for any signs that she knows what's been going on in my head and planned this little horse ride, or whether this is just some innocent coincidence.

"I'm sure they're busy," I say.

"Probably. They always are. And anyway, we'll see them later for Christmas Eve drinks."

Christmas Eve drinks!

You've got this, Hollie. It'll be just fine. You can control yourself. You do not need to suck the face off those alphas or grind your pussy against their groins – You can behave like a civilized, grown-up human being.

We ride further out to the northernmost pastures and then we double back around. We're almost back to the house when Annie looks up at the sky like she so often does and frowns.

"That doesn't look so good," she says, pointing out toward the east where a great big black storm cloud hunches on the horizon. "I wonder if that's coming our way. I better go tell Mom and Dad."

We pick up the pace, put the horses back in the stable, and then Annie's running up the steps, Dolly clambering along behind her and barking as Annie calls her dad's name.

"Have you seen that threatening-looking storm cloud in the distance?" she says to him, finding him in the kitchen.

He shakes his head.

"I'm thinking, if you want to go and get those last-minute groceries, we'd better go sooner rather than later." He walks to the back door, opens it, and peers up at the sky. His expression is so like his daughter's, it's uncanny.

"Yep," he says. "Better go now, before that storm sets in. Where's your mom?"

He goes off to find her, and Annie turns to me, taking my hands in hers and lowering her voice.

"I would invite you on this grocery trip, Hollie," she says, "but I wouldn't want to expose you to the manic behavior that possesses my dad at this time of year."

"What do you mean?" I say, giggling.

"He gets a bit frantic, a bit crazy, a bit worked up about Christmas dinner. We did the grocery shopping a week ago, but he's made another long list of things he thinks we've forgotten, which is why we've got to go back today." She rolls her eyes. "Come with us if you want, but seriously, if I were you, I'd stay at home, snuggle up with Dolly and Kenny, and drink eggnog. I think I'm going to need one or two by the time I get back."

I don't know if Annie's being genuine, or whether she wants to spend some time with her mom and dad alone around Christmas, but either way I'm happy to hang out on my own in the house. Some time I can spend steadying my nerves and decoding all these feverish feelings.

"I think I might bake," I say, not thinking about that apple pie I promised to make for Clay – the one he said he'd like to taste. "Your dad's done so much of the cooking. I'd like to make him something."

"Go ahead," she says. "But... I really wouldn't bother if I were you." She grimaces. "He's seriously possessive about his kitchen. One knife out of place, one smudge on the worktop, one splatter in the oven–" She drags her finger across her throat.

"Okay," I say. "Maybe I'll stick to the crocheting."

I fail to admit that I haven't yet started the crocheting project on account of, yeah, my horny brain.

It doesn't take long for Mr. and Mrs. Jackson and Annie to load themselves up in the truck and hurtle away. I guess they really are concerned about that incoming storm. I go settle myself in front of the television, hoping for a source of distraction, Dolly and Kenny hopping up onto the couch with me.

I will not succumb to this horniness. I will not succumb to this horniness.

I flick on the TV just as the first flakes of snow fall from the now dark sky above the house. I sit and watch them fall, drifting, floating, mesmerizing. For a moment, I completely forget about the flickering television in front of me, or the dog nudging my hand and demanding attention. Then, eventually, I'm drawn back to the love story playing out on the screen and get back to stroking Dolly's tummy.

When I glance back at the window almost an hour later, outside is thick with white, heavy snow. So much so I can't even see the stables and there's already a foot of snow piled outside the back window.

I wonder how far Annie and her parents got. I hope they make it to the shop.

I walk over to the window and gaze out, Dolly accompanying me and accessing the weather herself.

"It doesn't look so great, does it?" I mumble to her.

It's properly blizzarding now, a full-on snowstorm, and I can't help worrying about the horses, about Annie, about the cattle, about the three alphas up there in their cabin. I nibble on my lip and remind myself they're all experienced country folk. This probably isn't the first snowstorm that they've encountered. They're likely not freaking out at all. They'll probably be back in 45 minutes, laughing at me for panicking so much.

I go make myself a cup of hot chocolate and locate snacks for Dolly and Kenny and bring them back to the television. I find another Christmas movie to watch – this one involving some city girl who falls in love with a country man – but I'm only half watching. My eyes keep drifting to the scene outside the window. The storm doesn't seem to be weakening or clearing. If anything, the snow seems to be becoming impossibly heavier. And now I think if I stepped outside it would reach well over my knees.

I'm contemplating calling Annie and checking she's okay when my cell buzzes on the cushion beside me. I pick it up. It's Annie. The line is crackly.

"Annie," I say, "Annie, are you okay?"

"Hollie, just fine. We're just fine. But this storm's set in. It looks like it's not moving anywhere for the rest of the day."

"Where are you?" I say.

"We made it into town," she says. "We're perfectly fine, but it's too heavy for us to drive back right now. We're going to have to stay here."

"But it's Christmas Eve," I say.

"I know, I'm so sorry, Hollie," she says. "I should have dragged you with us after all. Are you okay in the house on your own?"

"Annie, don't worry about me, *I'm* worried about *you*. What will you do if you can't get home tonight?"

"At least ten different people have already offered to put us up for the night. We won't be sleeping in the truck."

The line starts to crackle again and I don't hear her next few words.

"Annie? Annie?" I say. "Are you still there?"

But the phone goes dead, and when I look at it, I can see I've lost all signal. Great. It must be down to the weather.

I type her a text message anyway in the hope it might get through, and then I snuggle up under the blankets and try my best to watch the movie.

It's just coming to an end – the heroine and hero smooching on screen and declaring their undying love for one another – when there's a large, thumping knock on the front door. I scream so loud I swear half the baubles on the Christmas tree smash.

Dolly leaps to her feet and barks and even Kenny's ears shoot up dead-straight.

I freeze.

This is how every horror movie I've ever watched starts off, right? The heroine by herself in the big house, trapped in the snowstorm, all alone, and then a knock on the door. There is no way in hell I am answering that door. It could be a bogeyman, or worse, it could be a yeti.

I hunker down in my blanket, close my eyes, and hope I imagined that thump. Except next thing I know there's a loud knocking on the large glass windows. I scream again.

Dolly barks like mad and Kenny starts thumping his back paw.

I know I shouldn't look to see what's out there, but I'm unable to help myself. And this is how every heroine dies. It's always their curiosity that gets the better of them.

Yeah, but I can't help myself. My gaze shoots that way and I scream a third time. Possibly the loudest. Forget yetis or mass murderers, there's an abominable snowman glaring at me through the glass doors.

Dolly, far more brave than I am, goes charging toward the window, ready to protect me from the creature who is, any moment now, sure to smash through the door.

Except, Dolly doesn't bark or growl or look intimidating in any shape or form. Instead, she jumps about excitably, her tail wagging like mad.

The snowman brushes snow from his face, and waves at us through the glass.

I almost cry with relief. It isn't a yeti or a bogeyman or a mass murderer. It's Clay, Nash, and Tucker, covered in snow and peering through the glass.

I untangle myself from the blanket and scurry their way, unlocking the back door and almost screaming again at the blast of cold, snowy air that comes hurtling right at me.

"Just came to check you were okay, Hollie," Clay says. "We heard the others got trapped in town and that you were here alone."

"Oh, you didn't need to do that," I say. "I'm hanging out with my new best pals." I gesture to Dolly who is busy sniffing Clay's boots and Kenny already dozing again on the couch. "You just gave me a bit of a scare, that's all," I press my hand to my still racing heart. Although I'm not quite sure if it's racing now from the shock and the fear and the scary atmosphere, or if it's racing because the three alphas in front of me are so startlingly good-looking it could set a girl to fainting. Especially when those three men are decked out in their winter gear, covered in snow, looking more manly than it's possible for three men to look.

"You sure?" Clay says, eyes darting around inside the living room. "Is the heating working alright?"

"Erm..." I say, having no idea.

"We'll start a fire for you, just in case it goes out." He marches inside, the other two following behind him. They kick off their boots and then they set to work around the fireplace, loading it full of logs of wood, kindling, and old pieces of newspaper. Then Clay strikes a match and the whole thing leaps up into flame, and the fire's soon roaring, toasty warm.

I'm not sure I've ever seen anyone build a fire so quickly and so effectively before, and I will now be squirreling that little image away in my brain alongside the tree cutting, the hay throwing, the horse grooming, and the kissing. Maybe Annie's right. Maybe I am just one big horny pervert.

"Fill the sink with water – and fill some bottles too," Clay tells me next. "Sometimes the pipes can freeze up if the heating goes out or we lose the electricity."

I nod, twisting my hands behind my back.

"Do you want to come in?" I ask them. The thought of being in this confined space with all three alphas sends my heart into a stuttering mess and my panties into an even bigger one. But, it doesn't feel fair to resign them to the cabin in this storm. I'm obviously only considering their welfare.

"We're off to check the cattle," Clay says.

"Check the cattle!" I screech. "You're going out in this!"

"Got to. The cattle are our responsibility and we can't risk them getting lost in a snow drift or suffocated up against a fence. We need to check they've got enough to eat and the water supply hasn't frozen over."

I look out toward the snow whirling outside the window. I can't imagine anyone making it through that. They'd be lost in a snowdrift.

"Will your truck even make it through?" I say.

"Truck, possibly not. The horses will, though," Nash says.

"You're taking the horses out in this?"

"The storm's easing. It's much more settled out there now. Perfect window of opportunity to go check on the cattle," Nash tells me.

And then I don't know what possesses me. Maybe it's my horny brain, or the big fright I just got, or the fact that I can't bear to think of the horses and the cattle out in the snow, but I say, "I could come with you. I could help."

The three alphas stare back at me in shock.

"How... how could you help?" Nash says, sounding puzzled.

"I'm a vet. I know about sick animals. And I imagine you're going to need all the help you can get."

"We're not taking you out in a snow storm, Hollie," Clay says.

"Why not," I scowl at him, "Because I'm a girl or because I'm an omega?"

"Because you're precious and I don't want you getting hurt or sick or injured."

My mouth falls open in surprise and I gape at him. Did he really just say that? Did he just confess he has feelings for me?

"I'm ... I'm precious?"

"To Annie," he clarifies, not quite able to meet my eye, "she'd never forgive me if I let something happen to you."

Of course. I'm seriously dumb. That's the reason.

"And *I'll* never forgive you," I snap, "if you leave me here worrying about the lot of you, all on my own, at Christmas time."

"It's still a no."

I stamp my foot in frustration. "Can everyone stop treating me like I'm made of glass! My mom died, that's all, you don't need to tiptoe around me, refusing to freaking kiss me or knot me or whatever me, because you're scared I might fall apart. And I'm an omega, not a porcelain princess. I've been looking out for myself for an awful long time. I am tougher than I look. I've wrestled misbehaving Great Danes and sedated boa constrictors."

Tucker visibly shudders. "I freaking hate snakes," he mutters.

"I held my mom's hand when she was sick, I nursed her when she was ill, I even organized her funeral all by myself. I'm not scared of a little snow storm. So let me come!"

Clay considers me, stroking his fingers over his stubbled chin.

"Let her come," Tuckers says, clearly won over by my argument.

"But have you ever ridden in thick snow before?" Nash says, clearly not liking the idea either.

I want to stick my tongue out at him and tell him I've ridden in plenty of snowstorms before, but obviously that would be one big fat lie, so I shake my head reluctantly instead.

"She can ride with me," Tucker says. "On my horse."

"Great," I say. "Then I'll come."

And before Clay Jackson can start arguing with me again or listing all the reasons why this is a stupid idea, I run off to find my newly acquired winter-weather clothing. I'm back in a matter of minutes, half convinced they'll have gone without me. But they haven't. They're waiting for me by the back door.

"You sure you want to do this, Hollie?" Clay says. "It's horrible out there. It won't be pleasant by any stretch of the imagination."

I shrug. I don't tell him that what else am I going to do – sit on my own watching TV like I've been doing for months? The only thing that will achieve is that sadness creeping in through the cracks and overwhelming me, especially on Christmas Eve.

I'm sick of that. I want to feel alive. I want adrenaline pumping through my veins. And, yes, if I'm totally honest, I want to spend time with the three of them – even if it is in a snowstorm.

"Come on then," Clay says. "Let's go."

And he leads the way out to where the horses are sheltering under the overhang of the barn. Tucker motions for me to mount Storm, and I do. Then he's following up after me, settling himself in the saddle right behind me, his arms coming to wrap around my waist and take a hold of the reins. The snow swirls angrily around us, slapping into our faces with a bitter coldness.

Tucker shakes the reins, clicks his tongue, and then we're on our way.

Chapter Nineteen

Tucker

Hollie Bright is right. She's not some teeny, tiny Omega princess. There's substance to the girl – curves and flesh and muscle.

And, fuck, even through all the layers of clothes I'm wearing and she's wearing, I can feel that substance as clear as day, because my body is pushed right up against hers, my arms wrapped around her waist as we ride on Storm through the dense snow.

It's not her build that makes her tough though – she's still an omega after all – teeny tiny compared to me and my baulking great pack mates. What makes Hollie tough is her big heart and her bravery – a bravery I'm not sure I recognized until today. She's a tough little cookie. And yeah, she is little, no matter what she says – she's still a whole foot shorter than I am. Luckily, Storm is the biggest and strongest horse that we have here at the ranch. The added weight, despite the brutal conditions, doesn't seem to be bothering him.

It's just as well she is tough because the storm kicks up again as we near the pasture with the cattle. The wind whips around our faces and the snow hits us like the sharpest of blades. The little Omega huddles in my arms, taking the full brunt of the elements. She doesn't complain, though. Like she said, she's tough.

Her words rattle around my brain. She's not scared of us. She's not scared of where things might lead between us – that's what she meant, right? She doesn't want us treating her like she might break any moment. The girl's withstood a lot. And she is still standing. I guess, in comparison to what she has been through, what are three asshole alphas?

"Okay there, sweetheart?" I ask as we cross the first pasture and reach the shelter of the trees. The weather's been unpredictable for the last few weeks, and we made the decision to move the cattle closer to home – easier to keep an eye on – and I'm thankful for that decision now. It means the ride is shorter.

"I'm okay," she says. "Although fuck, it's cold." She shudders in front of me, and I hug her more tightly.

"We're nearly there," I say. "Next field. That's where the cattle are."

We pass under the trees, the horses huffing with the exertion, clouds of cold air hanging around their faces and ours, and then we emerge into the next pasture. It's thick with snow, and it blows across like a curtain.

"They're in this field," I tell her. But the snow is so dense now it's impossible to see farther than a few feet in front of our noses, and so we can't spot them straight away.

"Should we spread out and look for them?" Nash asks.

"No," Clay calls back over the sound of the howling wind. "Better stick together."

I nod my agreement, and we take a right, deciding to circle the field in an anti-clockwise direction. Hopefully, we'll find the cattle soon.

We hear them before we see them – a low, bellowing rumble, barely audible above the fierce storm.

"Do you hear that?" Hollie says, twisting in my arms and looking at my face.

"I think they're in that direction," I call to the others, and we push on with the horses.

We find the cattle huddled together under the loafing shed, their backs to the wind.

"Are they okay?" Hollie asks.

"I doubt they're having the best Christmas Eve of their lives," I tell her, "but these girls, they're hardy."

I jump down from my horse and offer her a hand. She gives me a look and slides off easily herself, landing in the snow with a bounce. We stroll toward the herd. The old girls are usually a dark brown in color, but today their fur is matted with crusted snow, as if someone has iced them like cakes.

"They're pregnant?" Hollie says.

"Yep. Calves will come in spring," I tell her.

The cattle hear us coming and turn and start walking our way.

"They think we've got food, right?" she asks me.

"Yep," I say. "Sorry, girls, but we left plenty in the field yesterday." In fact, Clay and Nash are already looking for the hay bales, sprinkling it on top of the snow. "Come on," I say. "Let's check the water."

At the back of the shed, there are two troughs fed by the

pumps. "It's heated and insulated to stop them from freezing over in the winter but it's always worth checking. Besides, the water trough itself may have iced over," I explain. And I'm right – they have. There's a thick layer of ice sitting on top of the water, preventing the cattle from drinking.

I walk back over to Storm, pull a small pickaxe from the saddlebag, and stroll back over. The ice is thicker than it looks, and it takes me several swings to crack it. Then I use the other end of the axe to swirl it into the water, encouraging it to melt. Then I walk to the next one.

"Hey, tough girl," I say with a smirk. "Want to give it a try?"

She lifts her chin with determination. "Yep," she says.

I hand her the axe. She swings it right up above her head and then down again with a hard thwack. The blade of the axe lodges straight in the ice and refuses to move, and the propulsion has her losing her balance and skidding on the snowy ground. I'm there in a flash, righting her back on her feet.

"Sorry," she says.

"It's okay," I tell her. "Takes a bit of skill. Watch."

I unhook the axe from the ice and thwack it again. Then I hand it back to her. She copies my action and this time keeps her balance. The ice cracks, fissures running along its surface, and she sinks it into the liquid below with a satisfied smile.

"I did it," she says.

"I think you could do anything you set your mind to. Hollie Bright. You're right, you are tough, and I'm sorry if we haven't treated you that way."

She glances up at me. "I'm not always tough."

"Can I let you into a little secret?" I say, bending low so my mouth is by her ear.

"What's that?"

"I'm not always tough. And you may find this incredibly hard to believe, but neither is Clay Jackson."

"Oh my goodness," she says, giggling. "I think I might drop dead with shock."

"Please don't," I tell her. "Dead bodies are extremely hard to move and even harder to dispose of."

"Do you have experience?"

I wink at her, and she giggles again.

I tuck the axe into my belt and then I offer her my hand, noticing for the first time that she's shivering. "Come on," I say. "Let's go and find the others, give them a hand."

She stares at my outstretched palm. "Are we holding hands now?" she asks.

"Don't want to be separated in a snowstorm, sweetheart," I say with a grin. "Wouldn't want to lose you. Besides, you have a rather frequent habit of falling over."

She sighs. "I do. I've got two left feet."

"Wow," I say. "Is that true? I was beginning to suspect you were doing it on purpose."

"Why would I fall on my ass on purpose?" she asks, taking my hand in hers. We're both wearing gloves, so I can't feel the warmth of her hand, but it's still satisfying.

"On account of the fact I'd catch you, and I think you rather like that. Rather like being in the arms of a big, strong alpha."

"Hmm," she says. "I'll have to think about that one."

She smiles up at me, and I see her teeth are chattering and her whole body shaking.

"You're cold," I say.

"A little."

I frown. It's clear that's a blatant lie. She's a lot cold.

I stride over to the others who are still busy checking over the cattle.

"I'm taking Hollie back to the cabin before she catches hyperthermia."

"What? NO!" she screeches in horror.

But the other two take one look at the shivering little omega – shivering so hard she can barely stand – and nod their agreement.

"I'm not going," she says, snatching her hand from mine and crossing her hands over her chest in defiance.

"You either come willingly, little Omega, or I throw you over my shoulder and force you back to the cabin."

She narrows her eyes at me. "You wouldn't dare."

"Try me," I say with a jerk of my chin. She considers me and then with a sulky huff, concedes and starts walking toward Storm.

"I'll see you back at the cabin," I tell the others and then hurry after her, half concerned she'll steal my horse.

We're half way back across the field, when Hollie points something out in the distance. "What's that?" she asks.

I squint against the battering snow storm. "Looks like one of our girls has got separated from the herd." I yank on the reins and go investigate.

One lone cow, her stomach rounded with a young calf, stands lowing on her own, completely lost and disori-entated.

"It's lucky you spotted her, sweetheart," I tell Hollie, "She won't last long out here on her own like this."

"How are we going to get her back to the others?" she asks. Wrapped in my arms, she's not shivering as violently as she was, but it's clear she remains frozen. I need to do this quickly.

"Like this." I reach down to my saddle, unhook the coil of rope and then I swing it over my head. It's not easy in the battling wind, but I'm well-practised and lasso around the cow's neck on the first fling of the rope. Then I yank it tight and have the cow trotting along behind her as I lead her back to the herd. Clay unhooks the rope from her neck.

"Will she be okay?" Hollie asks.

"Don't worry, we'll get her warmed up," Clay says, already rubbing his hands over the cow's back, "you go get *yourself* warmed up, Hollie."

Nash tips his head back and looks up to the sky. "You know," he says, "I think it's clearing."

Turns out Nash is right. As we ride back to the big house, the wind drops and the snow settles until it's light, drifting through the air like the perfect Christmas scene.

I'm guessing the Omega sitting between my thighs agrees, because she coos and says, "This place is so darn pretty."

"Yeah," I say, "but it's a whole lot prettier with you in it."

I know what the others said. I know what they think.

Hollie Bright is vulnerable. Hollie Bright is grieving. Hollie Bright should be left well alone.

I also know what Hollie herself said back at the house.

Besides, I can't help myself. Her ass pressed up against me has made me harder than I've been in years, and now that the storm has settled, her scent is thick in the air again.

I can smell it – I can taste it in my mouth – that sweet, sweet honey.

She turns her head to look up at me. "You're a real sweet talker, Tucker Parker," she says. "Your tongue must be made from caramel."

"I have been described as charming once or twice in my time," I say with a smirk. Then, with an even bigger one, "Also, I've had plenty of compliments about my tongue."

"I suspect your tongue gets you into an awful lot of trouble."

I chuckle. "You have no idea, sweetheart. No idea at all. But if it could get me into trouble with you, it would be worth it."

"Maybe you should stop talking," she says, "and put that tongue to good use."

"Oh yeah? And how would that be?"

"By kissing me, for a start," she says.

And I do not need to be asked twice. I hold her in my arms, bend down, and kiss her lips. Luckily, Storm knows the way home. He's not about to bolt or throw me off, even if I am making out with a girl on his back. And so, with one hand lightly on the reins and the other wrapped around her waist, I kiss Hollie Bright – and I show her just how good my tongue can be.

When we break apart, Hollie smiles up at me.

"So," she says.

"So," I say.

"Annie and her parents are stuck in town on account of the snowstorm."

"Yep, they certainly are."

"Do you think they'll be coming home anytime soon?"

I shake my head. "There's at least four feet of snow out

there on the roads. They won't be coming home tonight, that's for sure."

"So," she says again.

"So," I repeat.

"We have the house to ourselves."

"We do, but I think I'd better get you to our cabin and warm you up, little Omega. It's closer."

And she smiles even more brightly and replies, "Yes, I think you better."

Chapter Twenty

H ollie

That kiss with Tucker may have been hotter than holy hell, but I'm freezing my ass off, and I'm utterly relieved when the alphas' cabin comes into view. I'm guessing Storm must feel similarly because he picks up his pace and we're outside the cabin in no time at all.

Tucker leads me straight inside, and has a fire roaring in a matter of minutes, leaving me to strip off my wet outer layers while he ensures Storm is warm and settled in the shed row barn. When he returns, I'm standing by the fire in just my woolly sweater, my panties and my socks. Luckily, the sweater is an over-sized one that falls to the top of my thighs, ensuring my modesty, but Tucker takes a good look at me anyway.

"It's very Christmassy in here." I point to the large decorated tree, the strings of lights and the evergreen garland string above the fireplace.

"Nash," he explains, "he's our design guru and he likes everything looking festive for the holidays. Do you like it?"

"I love it. Are you sure one of you isn't actually Santa and this is your grotto?"

"Definitely not Santa but more than willing to make your Christmas wishes come true, sweetheart." He winks at me. "Still cold?"

I've wrapped a blanket around my shoulders but my teeth are still chattering.

"A little," I tell him.

He frowns and then he's busy boiling a kettle and soon I have a steaming hot mug of tea in my hands and he's maneuvering me into an armchair in front of the fire and encouraging me to drink the tea down.

Usually, I hate feeling cold – it's not a sensation I'm used to having lived all my life in Rockview – but I'm more than happy to sit sipping my hot tea as I watch Tucker strip off his wet clothes, go around tidying away the equipment he'd taken out with them, checking the electrics, feeding the fire, and asking me frequently if I'm feeling warm yet.

"Almost," I say. "It's just my toes now."

I wiggle them in my thick socks.

"You've got cold feet?" Tucker says.

"You have no idea. I always have cold feet."

"Well, that's no good. It's the most miserable thing in the world, having cold feet."

"I know."

He drops to his knees before me, and then he's rolling down my right sock.

"What are you doing?" I say. "They're gonna get even colder."

"No, they're not."

He takes my first foot in his warm hands and rubs them.

"Oh," I moan. "That feels really good."

"Exactly."

He yanks off my other sock and warms that foot too.

"Better?" he asks.

"Yes," I say with a big smile.

He meets that smile with an even bigger one of his own. "How about your legs, sweetheart? Are they cold too?"

"A little," I say, sensing where this may be leading and more than happy to play along.

He shakes his head. "That just won't do."

He runs those big hands of his, warm and slightly calloused, up my calves, massaging them as he does. It's not exactly the most erotic action and yet his touch feels electric against my skin.

When his hands reach my knees, he glances up at me.

"How about the rest of you, sugar?"

"Definitely cold."

"Want me to warm up all of you?"

I bite down on my lip and nod. I don't think I've ever wanted anything more.

"If you change your mind–" he begins.

"I'll be sure to tell you, Cowboy."

He chuckles and then he's gliding his hands up the top of my thighs. I bite down harder on my lip when he reaches my hips and slides his hands down the inside of my thighs. I'm incredibly sensitive there and it's enough to make me shiver.

"There's one way I know of that will definitely get those cheeks of yours glowing," he says with a smirk as he strokes back up the inside of my thighs, reaching my panties.

"Oh yeah, what's that?"

He strokes his fingers along the gusset of my panties. I'm even *more* sensitive there and I jolt against his touch.

"I think you know," he murmurs, his voice now low and husky. He traces the outline of my panties with his fingertips. "You want me to stop, Hollie?"

"Absolutely not."

"Thank fuck for that." He groans and then he's hooking his fingers into the waistband of my panties and sliding them down my legs.

I'm sitting in front of a kneeling alpha with my pussy completely exposed to him and I'm not sure even my wildest fantasies have quite lived up to this.

He pushes against my knees, encouraging me to open my legs and then he stares right between them. You'd think I'd be cringing with embarrassment – usually I would be – but the look on his face is full of admiration, as if he's gazing upon some amazing piece of artwork, and it's a massive turn on. I can feel myself getting wet.

"Look at you slicking, Omega. Is that for me?"

"It's because of you," I mutter, my heart pounding with the anticipation of what he's going to do next.

"You have such a pretty pussy? Especially when it's all needy and desperate like this."

I bite my lip so hard, I'm surprised I don't draw blood. He strokes his hands all the way up my legs one last time and sweeps his thumb through my wet folds.

"You're dripping," he groans, examining his digit covered in my slick. "I have to taste you." And then he's leaning forward and dragging his tongue over me, swirling his tongue around my clit. The sensation is so intense it has me groaning too and gripping the arms of the chair, my head tipping backwards and my legs already shaking.

"You like that?"

"A lot," I whimper. It's been a long time since anyone's touched me intimately and to be honest, none of the men I was with before were any good at this. They were sloppy or lazy or just pretty lost, unable to tell where a knee cap started and a clitoris ended despite my best attempts at instructing them.

I can already tell that with Tucker Parker this won't be a problem. He needs no instructions at all. The way he's circling my clit in an achingly, teasing manner is too good for words. It has all the blood in my body rushing to my pussy and every nerve end tingling, waiting, hoping he's going to give me more.

He moans against me and that has me jolting, seriously close to the edge from just these simplest of attentions.

"You taste so delicious, Hollie. A million times better than I imagined. I could sit here and eat you out all day and all night."

He drags his tongue through my folds a second time, slurping all the slick that's gushing from my pussy up into his mouth and ending with a hard flick of my clit that has me seeing stars. Then he really goes to town, French kissing my pussy, sucking me up into his mouth before delivering devastating flicks to my clit.

I fall apart, everything inside me – all that tension, all that worry, all that grief – coming undone. I whine. I whimper. I curse. I thrash about on the chair, desperate to grind my pussy right into his wicked mouth. He's forced to hold me still with his firm grip, sending me right to the brink and then letting me free fall into ecstasy.

"Tucker!" I cry out as I come all over his face, way more messily than I ever have before. "Oh, God, Tucker!"

He doesn't stop. He flicks, licks and slurps me right through my orgasm and straight into a second until I'm begging him to stop because I don't think I can take any more, tears rolling down my cheeks and my body covered in a fine layer of sweat.

He rocks back on his heels, peering up at me with one of those heart-stopping smiles, my mess smeared all over his mouth and his chin.

"Warm again now, sweetheart?" he asks me.

I'm about to tell him that was the hottest experience of my life, when the cabin door swings open and Clay and Nash come marching through, stopping dead in their tracks when they spot Tucker kneeling in front of my bare pussy, the perfume of my slick thick in the air.

Chapter Twenty-One

Clay

I've never seen anything so mind-blowingly hot as my packmate – my oldest friend – kneeling between the bare thighs of Hollie Bright. My brain malfunctions. My cock stiffens. And for a moment I forget all my responsibilities and reservations. I think I almost forget my own name.

That is until Tucker stumbles to his feet, his mouth and his chin shiny with– is that slick? – looking suitably sheepish.

"What the hell is going on?" I snap.

"I know it's been a while since you've been with a woman–"

"It has?" Hollie says, cheeks bright pink.

"-- but I think you know," my friend says, licking all that delicious smelling mess from his lips.

"You're a fucking asshole," I growl. Has he forgotten

what we talked about? Our agreement to give this girl the space she needs?

"What's your problem?" Hollie says, snapping her legs closed and scowling my way.

"Clay and Nash are both in agreement," Tucker says, addressing Hollie but keeping his gaze locked on me, "that we shouldn't be messing around with you, Hollie."

"Why not?" she asks, clearly hurt and making *me* feel like the asshole and not Tucker.

"You only just lost your mom," I say softly. "You're vulnerable and–"

"I already told you," she says fiercely, "to stop treating me like you're scared you might break me." And then, before I understand what's happening, Hollie Bright is on her feet and marching toward me. She doesn't stop until she's right in front of me. I'm expecting a slap, or at least a firm talking to. Instead, she fists her hands into my wet jacket, lifts up onto her toes and kisses me hard on the lips. It lasts five deliciously long seconds. Then she snaps back her head, peers up at me with those piercing blue eyes and tells me, "I want this. I want you. The question is, do *you* want *me*?"

"Of course, I fucking do," I growl, dragging her right up against me and kissing her back, just as hard, just as passionately, just as hungrily as she kissed me. She melts into my arms and I slide my hand down her body, over her ass to the hem of her oversized sweater. Then, I glide my hands under that sweater, finding her pantiless and bare.

It tips me right over the edge. I have no more self control to give. I want Hollie Bright. I've wanted her for a very long time. No more waiting. No more reservations. I'm going to have her.

I groan into her mouth and hitch her up off the floor.

Automatically, she wraps her legs around me and, still kissing her mouth, I carry her straight through to the far room of the cabin. A room we built and decorated when we erected the cabin. A room that's never been used. A room that's been waiting for a moment like this.

As we step through and I kick the door closed behind me, she breaks off our kiss and tips back her head, gaze darting around the room – at the sky light above us (buried under snow), at the oversized bed with all its covers and cushions, at the plush carpet and curtains, at the fairy lights strung around the room, at the armchairs and sofa.

"Is this ... is this a nest?" she asks, eyes wide with wonderment – an expression that has my alpha pride well and truly stroked.

"Yes, it is."

"It's gorgeous," she purrs. She swings her gaze back to me and smiles ever so sweetly. "Are Tucker and Nash going to be joining us?"

"You want that?" I ask, almost afraid of the answer, afraid to wish for it as hard as I am.

"Yes, I want that, because I like all of you." My heart stutters in my chest and I'm forced to close my eyes and breathe. "Clay, is that a bad thing?"

"Fuck, no, it's the best thing." I open my eyes and smile at her.

"It is kind of fucked up though, isn't it?"

"It's natural, Hollie. You were designed to be a pack omega." Designed for us. I can't believe this is really happening. It's like all my Christmas wishes coming true all at once. "Have you ever done it with more than one person before?"

"No." The idea obviously turns her on because she whimpers, grinding her hips against mine. Fuck, this girl is needy and dripping with slick. She's every alpha's dream. "But I want that so badly."

"And we're going to give it to you, baby. But first," I swallow, "I'm going to fuck you. I'm going to get you ready, all nice and wet and pliant for the three of us. But also because, I'm fucking selfish, Hollie, and I want you to myself for just a little bit. Is that okay?"

"It sounds more than okay," she tells me. "It sounds perfect."

I place her down on her feet, shrugging off my wet coat and slinging it to one side. I left my wet boots and gloves at the front door and so I stand there in my damp pants, socks and sweater, unable to tear my eyes away from the woman in front of me - her caramel hair wet and disheveled from the storm, her cheeks rosy from whatever antics Tucker had been up to, blue eyes radiant.

"Erm Clay," she says, eying me in the same way I'm eying her. "What the hell is that?"

She points at my chest and I glance down at the sweater I'm wearing.

"It's my Christmas sweater." There's a picture of a cowboy boot in the middle with big red lettering that reads 'Howdy Holidays' above it. I hasten to add, I did not choose this sweater.

"Clay Jackson owns a Christmas sweater?"

"Annie and my mom insisted I get into the Christmas spirit. They made me wear it."

"And you, being a grown man and an alpha, had no choice but to comply."

"It's Christmas."

"And you're a softie."

"Sweetheart," I growl, finding the hem of her sweater again. "I'm definitely not soft."

"Thank all the Christmas elves and angels for that!"

"Can I?" I ask, tugging at the hem of her sweater. She nods and I pull it over her head, gently to allow her to thread out her arms, ensuring her chin doesn't snag on the head hole or her hair catch in the fabric. She has another top underneath as if she's a gift I get to unwrap. I lift this one over her head, finding a camisole underneath this time.

"How many layers are there going to be?" I growl, making her giggle.

Fortunately, the camisole turns out to be the last because when I remove it, I finally find a bra – Christmas red with a sprigs-of-holly design.

"And you had the audacity to criticize my sweater," I tut. "Do you always wear underwear that matches your name?"

"Doesn't everyone?"

"I never thought brown was a good look for underpants."

She giggles again. "It's just my Christmas bra. Don't you like it?"

"Like it, I fucking love it. I'd love it even more if it was decorating the floor."

She rolls her eyes because I bet the girl has heard that line more than once, especially as she has the most spectacular pair of tits known to man, a pair I can't help groaning at when she unhooks her bra and tosses it away.

"Fuck," I mutter, "can I?" I stagger toward her, arms outstretched. She nods and I take those perfect tits in my hands – soft and round and voluptuous. My cock strains in my pants and I can't help but lean down and bury my face between her breasts, soft against my cheeks and swimming in her scent.

"I've wanted to do this from the moment I met you."

"You mean when I sneezed all over you," she says with a ton of sarcasm, "and covered you in snot."

"When you sneezed and it made your tits jiggle in a way that fucking short-circuited my brain."

"Oh," she says, "is that really a thing?"

With difficulty, I extract myself from her tits and roll back up. "It is a very big thing. When your tits jiggle – when your ass jiggles too - it does things to me."

Her gaze flicks down to where I'm straining in my pants. "I can see." She arches an eyebrow, then to my absolute delight she shimmies her shoulders cheekily, making her tits bounce. My cock twitches.

"I need a closer inspection," she says, "to see if that did have the desired effect."

"I'm assuming you want to take a look at my cock, sweetheart."

"For science reasons, obviously."

"For science." I take a hold of my belt and start to unbuckle it, and, fuck me, this girl is perfect because the little thing actually licks her lips greedily. But then she seems to change her mind.

"Stop," she says. My hands freeze mid-motion. I'm an asshole – I know I am. But I know where the line sits between an asshole and a creep. I have a little sister. Consent is important to me and if she isn't in to this, if she wants to stop at any moment then–

"Let me do that, please," she says.

I can't help smiling, relief flooding through my over-stimulated body. "Be my guest."

She doesn't take a hold of my belt, instead she tackles my sweater first, lifting it over my head, and then my shirt, threading each button through its corresponding hole until the thing hangs open. It seems to take an eternity. I'm desperate to feel her hands on my body. I'm desperate for her touch.

She yanks the shirt down my arms and peels my thermal tank top over my head. Then she simply stands and stares, her hot gaze running all over me, so hot it's as if I can feel it against my skin.

"Jeez," she mutters, "pecs like those should be illegal." Her eyes flick up to meet mine. "Can you make yours jiggle?"

"You mean like this?" I flex one then the other, making them dance for her. Her eyes light up like a kid on Christmas day who's just discovered their stocking's been filled to the brim. And I feel exactly the same way when she reaches out to touch me – finally.

Her hands are warm, her touch tender. She glides her palms over my pecs and my abs skimming the waist of my pants and making me gasp. She doesn't stop there. She sweeps her hands back up my body and over my shoulders, and then she's walking around me, running her hands down my back. Here, she pauses, her fingertips exploring the scars that run down my spine.

"Is this from the accident?" she whispers, her voice serious now.

"From the surgery," I explain.

She presses a kiss to the highest one – right at the base of my skull. "Does it hurt?" she asks.

I close my eyes.

Does it hurt?

Nobody's asked me that in a long, long time.

They did at first, after the accident, after the surgery, during the long months of recovery and rehab. Then they stopped asking. I guess they just assumed – assumed because I was walking, riding, working again – that everything was the same as it had always been.

I consider lying to her but the situation feels too intimate for that.

"Yes," I say, "especially when the weather's cold like this."

I sense her nod behind me. "Living with that kind of pain would be enough to make someone pretty irritable."

"Grouchy, you mean," I say, turning to face her and capturing her in my arms.

"Does anything help to ease it?" Her expression is so earnest.

"Being with you," I murmur, "something about your scent seems to dissolve away the pain. Your kiss makes me forget it completely."

Without another word, she reaches up on her toes again and kisses me, fumbling with my belt and buckle. I take over the task – dropping my pants and my boxers to the floor. I press her toward me, my cock – hot and sticky – rammed against her soft belly.

"I want to melt all your pain away," she murmurs, kiss-drunk against my lips, "I want to make you feel so good ... Alpha."

She's never called me that before – in all the time we've known each other, we've barely acknowledged what we are – but the way she says it now – forget short circuit – it freaking rewires my brain.

"Yes, Alpha," I growl. "Your alpha." At least for today.

Her pupils dilate and it's clear what a good omega she is.

"I'm so tempted to have you ride me, Omega, and watch those perfect tits of yours bounce," I mutter just as drunk on her and her scent as she is on me. "But I have this pressing need to fuck you, and fuck you hard."

I step away to the bedside cabinet.

"Where ... where are you going?" she says, almost in alarm as if she misses the proximity of my body already.

"Protection."

"Oh," I hear her swallow. "Do we ... do we need it?" I halt and slowly peer over my shoulder at her. She shuffles on her feet a little nervously. "I'm on contraception and I got tested after my last break up. I haven't–"

"I haven't been with anyone for a while, Hollie. None of us has. We've been too busy working, concentrating on the ranch. But our last tests were all clear."

Relief floods her face.

"You're on contraception?" I ask her, hardly able to contemplate what she's offering here, what she's offering me. She nods. "And you want to do this without ..." She nods again.

"I want to feel you. All of you."

I sweep her up into my arms, carrying her over to the bed and tossing her onto the mattress.

"You seriously always wanted to fuck me?" she asks as I climb up onto the bed after her.

"Always," I growl, burying my face in her neck and sucking the fragile flesh there, inhaling and tasting and drowning in her sweet, sticky scent.

"Is that just an alpha and omega thing?"

"No, it's a you and me thing."

"I thought you hated me," she says.

"Hate?" I snort. "Why the hell would I hate you?"

"Okay, maybe not hate, but I thought I really annoyed the heck out of you."

Reluctantly, I pull back my face to stare down at her

expression. I thought it was obvious, the way I felt about her. I thought my every move and my every action must have betrayed me, and that she'd just chosen to ignore it.

"If I found you so annoying," I say, "then why did I find every excuse, every opportunity to be with you when you and Annie were living together at college."

She frowns, clearly not understanding what I'm telling her.

"I helped you girls move all your stuff out of your room at college at the end of that first year, remember? And I helped you move into that apartment you rented and out again when you left."

She frowns a little harder and nods. Her skin is so soft and warm against mine, and I can feel the heat between her legs. It's like an invitation. But I want to have this conversation first. I want to make her understand just how much I've been pining for her all these years.

"I thought you did that because you were helping Annie," she says. "Because you're her big brother."

"And the time I took you both out for food in your second year because you were desperate to try that new Thai restaurant. And the time I took you grocery shopping when you were broke. The time I drove through the night to deliver tissues and chicken soup when you got sick with the flu."

"Again, I thought all that was for Annie."

I shake my head. "It was my way of finding excuses to be with you. To spend time with you."

"You never told me," she says.

"I didn't think you'd be interested," I admit. "I'm an alpha, and I remember one of the first things you said to me …"

All the blood rushes to her face and she morphs into a

tomato-red color in the dim light. Her hands fly up to cover her face.

"Oh my goodness," she says. "What did I say?"

"Something along the lines of, 'Urgh, an alpha,'" I say, imitating her voice and all the disdain her first words to me had betrayed.

"I didn't!" She peeks through her fingers. "Did I?"

"You did," I confirm.

"I think it's because you surprised me. I opened that door to our room that first time we met. Do you remember? And I wasn't expecting you there. It scared me half to death. You can be pretty darn intimidating, Clay Jackson, and I didn't have much experience with alphas – definitely not many positive ones. But also your scent – it kind of hit me between the ovaries and nearly had me slicking on the spot."

"You like my scent?" I say.

"Your scent is the most delicious thing I've ever smelled."

And then, to my surprise, she lowers her hands, reaches up, and drags her tongue up the column of my throat, her eyes rolling back in her sockets as she does.

"Chocolate brownies," she says. "You know how often I've eaten chocolate brownies and imagined you?"

I kiss her then – hard and passionately, stroking my tongue against her. Then I'm shifting her legs open with my knees, finding the hot heat between her legs, and sinking into her.

She's wet with slick, but even still there's a little resistance, and I pause halfway inside her to kiss her mouth again, to kiss her throat, to inhale her scent, to lift her leg and open her up further. When she's moaning and whimpering and her walls are relaxing around me, I sink even deeper inside her. All the way. And the feeling is so intense, so beautiful, so wonderful, I can't believe this is reality. I have to stop, close my eyes, and pinch myself, because it's not a dream. I'm here with Hollie Bright. My cock deep inside her pussy, resting between her legs, staring down at her beautiful face.

"Alpha," she whimpers beneath me.

"Just one moment," I tell her. I need to commit this moment to memory.

"I need you to move," she says. "You promised to fuck me."

I open my eyes and chuckle. I can't help it. Hollie Bright is needy, greedy, and I think I love her all the more for it.

I promised to fuck her hard. I wanted to fuck her hard. But now I'm here in this moment, I want it to last forever. I want to drag it out and enjoy the feeling of Hollie Bright's soft, warm heat wrapped around my cock.

I slide from her achingly slowly, torturing both her and me, and then I grind back into her just as slowly, just as torturously. She moans, her lower lip trembling. The pulse in her throat flutters. She takes a grip of my shoulders, nails sinking into my flesh.

"Alpha," she groans.

I wrap my arms around her too, cradling her against me, our skin flush together. I grind again and again and again. And she writhes underneath me, a sensitive little thing, her skin turning hot and sticky in my hands.

"You like that?" I ask her.

"More than I can say," she murmurs.

And so, even though this pace is killing me, I retain my control. I grind slowly, using the whole of my body to sink as deep inside her as I can. And then she's coming in my arms. I feel the tension rising up her spine, feel her muscles tighten, coiled like a spring. And then, with one final grind, she falls apart. Her body goes slack. It jolts with pleasure. Her head tips back. I kiss her neck, her chin, her mouth, as she mutters my name as her skin flushes a sweet rosy color.

"You're so beautiful when you come, Hollie."

I think that's the most beautiful thing I've ever seen – more beautiful than the sunrise over the mountains on a spring morning, more beautiful than the sun setting over the snow-blanketed pastures in the winter, more beautiful than the big blue sky that shines above the ranch on clear days when only the wispiest of clouds float above us.

Hollie Bright is the most beautiful thing I've seen on this earth, and she's most beautiful when I'm holding her in my arms and making her come.

It tips me over the edge. My alpha instincts take control. I turn feral.

"I'm going to fuck you hard, and I'm going to knot you."

"Clay," she mutters. "Please. Yes. Knot me."

I fuck the Omega hard on the mattress until she's screaming my name a second time, and I'm coming inside her bare cunt, filling her with my seed, and my knot is expanding.

Her pussy walls clench around me and her nails sink so deep into my shoulder I'm sure she's marking me with them.

And then:

"Oh God," she mutters. "Oh God, that feels – that feels –"

And then this little Omega, this truly wonderful miracle of an Omega, comes a third time as I knot her pussy – knot her pussy for the very first time.

Chapter Twenty-Two

H ollie

I've swapped tales with enough omegas, read enough online forums, and studied enough biology textbooks to know that an alpha's knot is meant to be the most incredible, mind-blowing, and downright erotic experience possible for an Omega – one I'd never experienced. Sure, I have my dildos with the fake knots – the ones that vibrate, that pulsate, that even expand to imitate an alpha's. They never really did anything for me. And I thought all those other Omegas, those online forums and those textbooks, had seriously exaggerated – big-time fake news – to try and convince us omegas to hook up with alphas despite their pushy natures, grumpy attitudes, and self-centered ways.

Turns out I was wrong.

I was wrong big-time.

At first, I don't realize. Clay holds me tight in his arms,

his cock jerking inside me and hot liquid flooding my pussy. He tells me he's going to knot me, and I hold my breath and wait. I feel a slight pressure at the entrance to my pussy and my heart sinks. It's nothing special. No better than all those stupid dildos.

But the thing is, it doesn't stop there.

It keeps expanding. The stretch is both alarming and, at first, even a little painful. But that's the delicious nature of it – the pain and the pleasure, like day and night, like sweet and sour, like hot and cold, mixing together, one swirling into the other, and soon the pleasure swamps through my body, drowning out all the pain.

His knot locks firmly into my pussy.

It's so intense. For a moment, my vision whites, all the noise in my head stops. All I am is sensation. And the sensation right now is pleasurable. Every nerve end in my body must be singing, and I'm sure I'm floating somewhere near the ceiling, maybe somewhere altogether heavenly.

When finally my never-ending orgasm stops, I drag open my eyelids, the world blurry for several seconds until Clay Jackson's handsome face finally comes into focus. He's watching me with those sky-blue eyes of his, so dreamy. I think they're the thing about him I like most. Well... maybe not *the* most. His cock and his knot are most definitely my favorite parts of the man built like an adonis.

"Good?" he asks me.

"So good," I mutter. "Please do that to me again and again and again. In fact, never stop doing that to me."

He chuckles. "You're going to have to wait a little bit of time for my knot to deflate before I can do that again, Omega. You're not in heat, and I'm not in rut."

The mention of those two words – loaded as they are – has both of us shuddering, and he growls, lowering his head to suck on my neck and sending me into more clouds of bliss.

I've never shared a heat with an alpha before, I've never wanted to. Now I most definitely want to share it with him. I'm just not sure how to ask. Because we haven't established what this is. Is it just a one-time thing? A holiday hook-up? A Christmas fling?

"I bet you're beautiful in heat, Omega."

"I am most certainly not," I tell him. "I'm a sweaty, sticky, disgusting mess."

"That sounds frankly amazing."

And I giggle as he rolls us onto our sides, shifting me until I'm comfortably curled up against his chest, his cock still knotted securely in my pussy. I could easily drift off to sleep now – sedated, content, and thoroughly well fucked.

But there's a firm and rather insistent knock on the door before my eyes have fluttered shut.

"I think my pack mates may have lost patience with me, Hollie," Clay admits, tickling his fingers up and down my bare back.

For a moment, lost in Clay Jackson's arms and all the delicious things he was doing, I'd forgotten about the two hot pack mates. But now I get a whiff of their scents, and something stirs inside me.

"Can we let them in?" I ask Clay.

"That's up to you."

I shuffle in his arms, bringing the bed sheet up over my body because I'm a little shy and a little nervous. But I want this. I want this a lot.

Clay is correct. I'm an omega. I was designed for a pack. One alpha is frankly not enough. So I remember what I told them about being tough. I need to live up to those words. I'm going to grow a pair of ovaries (a pair of ovaries that are more than happy with the current situation in which we find ourselves) and take what I want for Christmas. This pack.

"Come in," I tell them.

The door flings back almost immediately and Tucker's storming inside, Nash right on his heels.

I guess it's been pretty obvious what Clay and I have been up to. I wasn't exactly quiet. In fact, for the first time in my life, I was outrageously noisy during sex. Usually there's a part of me that's self-conscious – too aware, wondering how I look, how I sound, how I smell. But this time, I was too lost in the moment to care about any of that.

So I'm not surprised when Clay's packmates spot the two of us in bed together, and neither of them look surprised by what they've found. In fact, if anything, they look pleased.

"You been having fun?" Tucker asks me with an incredibly sexy lopsided grin.

"Uh-huh."

"Sounded like it," he says. "And he knotted you?"

"He did," I say.

"Your first time," Nash says, sliding off his glasses and folding in his arms. "You realize now what you've been missing out on."

"She wants me to knot her over and over again," Clay says, with a fair bit of pride in his voice.

"Actually," I correct him – which has disappointment momentarily shining in his eyes, "I'd like *all* of you to knot me over and over again."

I can feel Clay's knot deflating between my legs, and I wonder if, like I'm a pack Omega, he's a pack Alpha and his cock knows how to share. I wriggle free from his arms and, with the sheet still tucked under my arms, roll to sit up.

"Are you happy to oblige?" I ask them both.

Tucker winks at me. "I'm at your service, ma'am."

Nash simply stares at me and murmurs, "There's nothing I'd want more in this world."

"Good," I say, feeling the mattress shift beside me as Clay also rolls up to sit. "But there's one problem I see with this arrangement."

All three of their scents spiral in the air momentarily, signaling alarm that I have spotted a potential problem. What does that mean? That we're already highly in tune with one another? And does that mean we were meant for each other?

"What problem?" Tucker asks.

"Your packmates –" I point to Tucker and then to Nash "– are wearing far too many clothes."

I barely finish my sentence before Tucker has stripped most of the clothes from his body. His skin, despite the short winter days, is sun-kissed, and a swirl of ink runs over his chest and around his shoulders. The fuzz of hair that skims down his belly to his cock is darker than the blond locks on his head and a lot curlier. His cock itself is just as big as his packmate's, although it curves at a slightly different angle.

Nash takes more time undressing, his chestnut eyes locked on me the whole time as he carefully folds his sweater, his socks, his shirt, and then his pants in a neat pile. Tucker's practically bouncing on the soles of his feet by the time Nash finally – *finally* – slides his boxers down his thick thighs.

"Jeez, man," he mutters.

Nash's cock is hard too, and the little Omega inside me buzzes with pride. I did that. Just the thought of being with me is making them hard.

I'm not disappointed to find that Nash's cock is just as

big as his packmates', although it does provide me with some technical considerations.

I nibble on my lip as Nash and Tucker stalk toward the bed. "How is this going to work? Because … " I point to the two cocks striding my way. "There's no way– "

"Yes, there is," Clay growls beside me.

I snap my head in his direction. "You don't know what I was going to say."

"I do. You think, because we're big, you won't be able to take us all. And I'm telling you, you will."

I shake my head. Clay was big enough – he'd had to coax and cajole me to open up to him. He hadn't been able to fit all the way inside me at first.

"You're an Omega," Nash states matter-of-factly. "Your pussy was made to take knots. It was made to take more than one cock."

I'd forgotten how frank and how ridiculously dirty Nash's words could be. I'd also forgotten the effect they could have on me. I feel slick sliding from between my legs. The smell of it is sticky and sweet in the air, and the other two alphas are scrabbling up onto the bed.

"Hi," I say when I find myself in the center of a circle of very naked, very hot alphas.

Honestly, forget the wood-chopping, forget the hay-bale throwing, forget the horse grooming and every other slightly insignificant, minor erotic event that's ever happened to me in my whole entire life, because this blows everything out of the bedroom.

"Hey there," Tucker replies. "Fancy meeting you here – in your nest."

"What do you mean?" I say.

"It's yours now," Clay says.

And I know they're just words – words said to a girl

they're about to do frankly dirty, obscene things with – but it still has my heart fluttering. I'd love a nest like this. I'd love a nest that was built for me with love and attention. It's crazy, but it's as if these men knew what I wanted before even I did, because frankly there's nothing about this nest that I would change.

"So how exactly are we going to–"

But I don't finish my words because Tucker has hold of my shins. He yanks them down the bed so that I'm falling onto my back and then he's pinning my legs open.

"Nash," he says, "make our girl come."

"Yes," I say, "please do, Nash."

Nash leans over me, placing a sweet kiss to my lips first and then trailing those kisses down my throat, over my breasts, down my ribcage and my stomach until he reaches the apex of my thighs. There, he takes a deep lungful of my scent.

"I can smell your sweet slick, Omega. And I can also smell Clay deep inside your pussy."

Again, I wonder how an alpha who loves reading regency romance ended up with such a dirty mouth. And I don't think I appreciate just how dirty that mouth is until it's pressed right on my clit and is doing incredibly dirty things to me.

I'm already incredibly sensitive from the orgasms Tucker dragged from me with his tongue and from the orgasms Clay forced from my body with his cock and his knot. It takes very, very few flicks of Nash's dirty tongue and sucks of his dirty lips to have me falling apart all over again, thrashing on the bed as I sink my hands into his long, floppy locks and tug on them in a way that has him growling against me.

"She's so beautiful when she comes," Clay says,

brushing damp locks of hair from my face and then bending to kiss me sweetly on the lips, as his packmate continues to torture me between my legs.

And then I feel Tucker's mouth too on my breasts, skimming his wet tongue around the sensitive flesh of my nipples until they're crinkling and hardening, and then he's sucking them into his mouth, nibbling them between his teeth and flicking me with his tongue in just the same way Nash is flicking me with his.

And now I understand – now I understand what it's like to be a pack Omega, to have the attention of three alphas at once, all on me, to be their complete and utter focus. It's intense. In fact, I don't think I actually possess the words – I'm not sure any dictionary does either – to explain just how it feels, except that it's incredible. Utterly, fantastically, supremely incredible.

Soon, it's not only their mouths on my body; their hands are there too, exploring and touching. Nash's hands skimming up and down the soft flesh of my thighs. Tucker's hands coming to wrap around my waist, and Clay's coming to grip my throat. Their actions become more frenzied and more passionate, as if they're feeding ravenously on my body, as if they can't get enough of the way I taste and I feel.

And I admit it's the same for me. I can't get enough of this. Yes, I could die in this moment and I'd die one very happy, satisfied Omega – except I'm not quite satisfied enough, because as they wring another orgasm from my body and my pussy clenches around nothing at all, I moan, complain, and bitch about the fact I don't have a cock inside me or a knot.

"We'd better see to that then, hadn't we?" Tucker says, my nipple leaving his plush lips with an obscenely wet pop.

Nash murmurs his agreement, and then he's emerging

up from between my legs, his face just as filthy as his pack-mate's was several moments ago, my slick shining all over his chin and his lips.

Tucker pulls me up onto my knees, kissing me as his two packmates watch, and then turns me so my back is facing him. He's kneeling behind me, and he lifts me up onto his lap, his hot, hard cock nudging between my folds. He has a firm grip on my waist and he lifts me high up onto my knees, positions himself, and then drags me firmly onto his cock.

I cry out, my head tipping backward and coming to rest on his broad shoulder. His scent swims around me, encapsulating me in a safe, warm blanket of pine and forest. He nuzzles at my neck, holding me to him as we both catch our breaths. Then he's lifting his head and addressing his packmate.

"Nash," he says. "I'm going to fuck her now, and I want you to continue what you were doing."

"What?" I say.

"Nash is gonna eat you out, sweetheart, while I fuck you."

I try to work out how that's possible, but then Nash is flipping back down on his stomach, his hands resting on my thighs, his mouth between my legs again. He flicks at my clit as Tucker lifts me up, dragging his cock from me until only the tip remains, and then slamming me back down as Nash sucks me into his mouth.

My brain actually explodes inside my skull. All the molecules in my body rearrange, and after this nothing will be the same again. I'm spoiled – spoiled for all future relationships and every new man – except, even as that thought enters my head, I dismiss it immediately. I don't want to be with anyone else. I know it's early. I know I've only known these men for just a handful of days. I know this is the first time we've gone to bed together, and yet I can't see myself wanting anyone else ever again.

I cry out as Tucker's fingers grip me firmly and he increases his pace, slamming me down onto his cock harder and harder, Nash flicking me harder too, until stars streak across my vision and I come.

I come, and as I do, my gaze connects with Clay across the bed. He's sitting there watching me – watching me be fucked by his two packmates, watching me fall apart completely – and the look on his handsome face is so beautiful, I think I may be in love.

Chapter Twenty-Three

Tucker

The Omega convulses and squeezes around my cock as my packmate feeds on her pussy, and I'm done for. I wanted to make this last forever, to have the little thing bouncing up and down on my cock, her full, round breasts in my hands, her scent in my nose, and her pretty head resting on my shoulder. But I can't take any more. I can't handle how good it feels.

So I force her down into my lap, hold her there as my knot inflates and she squirms and wriggles, and I'm coming so hard, for a moment I think the effort of it has blinded me – bright white light streaking across my vision. And then she's relaxing in my arms, mewling like a little kitten, coming again because my knot feels so good to her. Her pussy squeezing around it is the best thing I've ever experienced in my life.

I groan. "Fuck, that's good."

She collapses against me – sweaty and panting and beautiful – and I lick my tongue up her throat, behind her ear, tasting that sweet honey mixed now with a little salt.

"You're so good, Omega. So good."

Nash rolls away from the two of us, ending up on his back with his hands flung over his head. "Shit," he mutters. "That was incredible."

The Omega looks up at me from where her head still rests on my shoulder, and I can read what she's asking me in her eyes. My cock deflates automatically, like it's already taking orders from this Omega, and fuck – I think it will. I think it will be at her beck and call from now on.

The Omega wriggles free from my arms, knocks forward onto her hands and knees, and then she's crawling toward Nash. He doesn't notice her come at first – his eyes are shut, his chest heaving – but then he must feel the shift of the mattress, must hear her panted breath, must catch her vibrant scent in his nose. He lifts his head and watches her crawl nearer.

"Hollie," he says.

The little Omega simply smiles at him as she crawls up his body, pressing kisses to his skin as she does – over his thigh, his hip bone, his stomach, the center of his chest, his shoulder, his neck, his mouth. Then she's hovering above him. Between her legs is a mess of spit and slick and come sliding down her thighs. It looks fucking dirty.

"Haven't you had enough yet, Hollie?" I ask, teasing her, because the number of orgasms the girl has had in the last hour must be a world record.

She shakes her head vehemently, her eyes still locked on Nash.

"Hollie, perhaps you ought to–" he begins.

But she leans forward, capturing his hands in hers and pinning them to the mattress. "I haven't had enough," she says. "Not nearly enough."

She lines herself up with my packmate's waiting cock, and then she sinks down onto him. She's seriously wet and pliant, and she slides easily down his thick cock. And all I can think about is when she's ready to take more than just one of us at a time.

Nash groans. His eyes roll back in their sockets, the muscles on his stomach twitch, and his toes curl.

"She feels good, right?" I ask him.

"So wet, so tight, so perfect," he answers.

And then I receive possibly one of the best little shows – one of the most beautiful views – of my life, because I sit on the bed and watch the little Omega bouncing up and down on my packmate's cock, her tits and her ass jiggling as she does, her skin flushed a rosy pink, her caramel-colored hair wild around her head, and all sorts of delicious noises rushing from her mouth.

Nash is meant to be the sensitive one in our pack – the one who likes reading and spending all his spare time with the horses. He's the one that would nurse a baby calf through the night. He's the one who insisted that rabbit ought to live in the main house and not out in a hutch in the cold. To see him, you'd never believe the dirty filth that can stream from that man's mouth. You have to hear it to believe it. And, oh shit, do I hear it now. The things he says, the way he says them, would have even a porn star blushing.

"Look at her – what a good little Omega she is, Tucker. Look at her bouncing – up and down, up and down – on my cock, Clay. Look at her rubbing her pussy up and down me, making herself slick, slicking all over my thighs. Smell how filthy she is, full of your seed. Look how much she loves this."

It seems Nash's filthy words do something to our Omega, because soon her pace falters. She falls down onto Nash's chest, and then she's jolting, twitching, squirming as another of those orgasms overtakes her.

"I can take more," she whimpers.

"Seriously," Nash asks, gazing up into her face.

"I want to try."

"Shit," I mutter, peering across to Clay. There will be a time when this omega can take all three of us at once but that time isn't tonight. Two of us, though, that's a possibility. The question is, which of us? "You," I tell my oldest friend. He's clearly and secretly been pining after this girl for years.

"You're sure?" he asks.

"Yeah, but get your ass moving before I change my mind."

Clay maneuvers himself over the bed, positioning himself above Hollie and Nash. He lines himself up with her pussy, already stuffed full of Nash's cock.

"We've waited a long time, Omega. A long time for a moment like this."

He grunts and buries his cock deep inside the Omega's cunt, all three of them wild with the feeling.

For one moment, our world is panted breaths and racing heartbeats – damp hair, sticky skin, filthy scents, and messed-up sheets. Nobody moves.

And then Clay's lifting his hips and sinking back into Hollie, making both the omega and our packmate groan with pleasure. It's clear how wild it sends them all and Clay only manages a handful of thrusts before Hollie's coming again, Nash straight after her.

There's no way the omega can cope with more than one

knot, so Clay pulls out of her pussy, grunting as he paints her skin with ribbons of come.

The three of them collapse down in one sticky, hot mess on the bed, limbs tangled. I wish I could take a picture. I wish I was an artist and could paint. Because they look incredible. I lie down beside them.

For a while we're all silent, catching our breaths and I'm sure each one of us is reflecting on what's just happened between us, that each of us has come to a realization. This is how it's meant to be between us. This is what we were meant to do. There is nothing better than this.

Hollie speaks first. "You said you'd waited a long time to do that. Was this the first ... I mean, I thought that... you're a pack and–"

"We've never shared an Omega before," Clay tells her.

"You expect me to believe that, Clay Jackson?" she says, with a teasing smile on her face.

"It's the truth."

"I'm glad." She snuggles in his arms. "Then it's special for you too, and you'll always remember it."

"Of course we'll always remember this," Nash says.

"You're making it sound," I point out, "like this is the only time we're going to do this, Hollie Bright. I missed out this time. But I'm definitely sharing you next time."

"Well," she points out. "I live in Rockview and you live here in Silver Creek–"

"Move in with us," Clay blurts out.

"Wha– " she says, almost bouncing off the bed. However, there's one big, inflated knot – Nash's – locked in her pussy and she can't go anywhere. I see now why biology did this. I don't want this Omega wriggling away from us. I want to hold her close, feel her heart thumping against my chest, drown in her sweet scent, nibble at her skin.

"Yeah, come live with us," I say. "Never leave us. Stay in this nest forever, and we can do this every day, all day, forevermore."

"Erm..." She giggles. "How about the ranch? The cattle? The horses? If you're here fucking me all day, who's gonna look after them?"

I groan, because I can't even pretend that we could just dismiss all that. Comes with the territory – comes with being an alpha – fucking responsibilities.

"I'll fuck you every night, then," I say. "And every morning."

"That does sound amazing," she murmurs.

And I can tell she thinks we're not serious, that it's just one of those things people say when they're in bed together. But that's because she doesn't know my packmate. Clay wouldn't say it unless he meant it.

I glance his way. He's watching us. "Tell her."

"Hollie," he says, capturing her attention again. "Come live with us. Come be ours."

Her brow crunches up. She tilts her head to one side. "We barely know each other."

"We've known each other for ten years," he says.

"Yes, but–"

"In all that time, I've known you were the one. I just didn't realize that you could feel the same way. But if you do, then what's stopping us?"

"My life in Rockview," she says. "There's my job, my apartment, Ted."

"Ted!!" we all say at once.

"Who's Ted?" Nash growls. "Because if there's another man, I am going to hunt him down and I will kill him." Maybe that's the knot in her pussy talking, because our sensitive, dirty-talking packmate rarely hurts a fly. But I understand his reasoning. If there's a man standing between us and Hollie Bright, I will take him out.

"Ted is my goldfish."

The three of us all let out audible sighs of relief.

"A goldfish," I say. "You own a goldfish."

"Yep."

"Goldfishes are pretty portable in my experience," Nash points out. "He could come live with us here."

"But ... there's still my job and my apartment and ..." She trails off, because her best friend's not in Rockview anymore, and neither is her mom. And we're here, willing to love her, willing to look after her, willing to be hers – if she'll have us.

"You could get a job in Silver Creek easily," Nash informs her. "They're always looking for vets in the area. As for the apartment, we're building a house."

"Hollie, we'll build it exactly how you want it," Clay offers. "You can have all the pink bathrooms and all the bookcases your heart desires."

She shakes her head in disbelief. "This is crazy," she says. "You're crazy."

It is crazy – and not like us at all. Especially Clay and Nash. They're rational, sensible, realistic. Sure, Clay's known Hollie a long time, but me and Nash haven't. We don't know if there are things that would irritate us about each other, those little niggles that would build up in time and drive us all nuts. We don't know if the Omega from Rockview would find Silver Creek too cold, too vast, too empty. We don't know whether we'd get bored with each other, whether we'd run out of things to say, whether the sex, the attraction, the heat would all fade away.

And it is crazy. And maybe I'm crazy. But I just don't think any of that matters. I don't think any of that will happen. I have a feeling about Hollie Bright. I've had it since I laid eyes on the little Omega and inhaled her scent. Maybe this is one of those Christmas miracles – the ones you read about in Christmas stories. Finding 'The One'. The Omega you were meant to be with. Maybe I knew that at the moment her honey scent tickled my nose and every single cell in my body took note, as if something special had entered the room.

I pull the blankets up around us and we snuggle together in the warmth as Clay goes to make us hot drinks and winter snacks. Soon he joins us in the bed too, and we talk together in whispers, staring up at the large skylight above us buried under several feet of snow and blocking out the sky.

And yet, I'm sure by now, it's dark outside.

Soon it will be Christmas Day.

Chapter Twenty-Four

Hollie

I was expecting this Christmas Eve to be my worst. It's now lining up to be my best by a long stretch. Better than that Christmas Eve I woke up convinced I'd caught sight of Santa rustling around in my stocking. Better than the Christmas Eve I woke up in the middle of night, unwrapped all my presents, and found Princess Celestial with her sparkly wings and rainbow-colored mane sitting in my stocking. Better than the Christmas Eve I kissed my high school crush under the mistletoe.

Because this Christmas Eve I have more orgasms in one night than I've had in the entirety of my life up until this point. More orgasms in one Christmas Eve than I've had in my 30 years on this planet. And not just any orgasms. Not piffling, crappy, little pathetic ones. Mind-blowing, earth-shattering, universe-defying orgasms. I should be destroyed, exhausted, and probably unable to walk. Instead, I'm lying on a bed in a snowy cabin surrounded by the three hottest alphas on the planet; my blood buzzing, my skin tingling, and a seriously big smile spread across my face.

It may only be the early hours of Christmas Day, but we've already exchanged gifts with one another over and over again. I've sucked their cocks, they've eaten my pussy, they've fucked me and licked me and fingered me and had me every way I think is possible.

And then there are the words they said to me last night, asking me to stay, to be theirs forever. We've talked about it some more and I don't know if I've completely lost my mind, if the grief and everything else that has happened has warped all my common sense, but I'm seriously tempted. First things first, though, we're going to start with dating. Long-distance dating.

If I think I'm going to enjoy this moment and make it stretch all the way into Christmas, though, then I'm given a rude awakening by the blast of a 5 a.m. alarm.

"What the heck?" I say, nearly tumbling straight out of the bed.

"Time to get up, sweetheart," Tucker says, as the three of them leap out of bed elegantly, not even attempting to snooze their alarm or draw the blankets over their heads.

"But it's so early."

"It's morning," Clay says.

"And Christmas Day," I point out.

"Happy Christmas, Hollie," he says, helping to pull me up and right me on my feet, pressing a kiss to the crown of my head.

"Can't we snuggle?"

"The cattle need checking on," he tells me, "and the

horses. And we left Dolly and Kenny overnight. I need to check on them too."

"It's so early," I continue to protest, but they ignore me, and soon I'm wrapped up in all my winter layers again, a plate of freshly cooked eggs shoved underneath my nose. I attempt to sulk about the situation, but it's hard when I'm being fed by alphas, cuddled by alphas, snuggled by alphas, and kissed by alphas. And soon I'm outside. It's still dark, the morning winter sun only just crawling toward the horizon. But it must have stopped snowing hours ago. Everything is still and silent and perfect outside, the snow fresh and crisp and undisturbed. I have the very big desire to go stomping through it or to drop down onto my back and make snow angels, but Tucker has me back on Storm and soon we ride toward the big house as the sun's rays creep across the untouched snow.

They drop me off with instructions to check on Dolly and Kenny and promising they'll be back after they've checked on the cattle and horses. I make a half-hearted attempt to argue that I want to come with them again, but after I nearly froze to death yesterday, I'm pretty glad when they refuse to let me join them.

Dolly and Kenny are extremely pleased to see me, although both sniff at me for an incredibly long amount of time.

"Okay, guys," I say to them as I shake out food into Dolly's bowl and slice up carrots for Kenny. "So you worked out what happened. Just don't go blabbing to Annie. Not yet, anyway."

Because there's just one big flaw in this potentially happy-ever-after plan, and it isn't Ted the goldfish.

Annie.

She said the idea of me and her brother together was

gross. It definitely goes against some of the fundamental rules of Girl Code. You shouldn't look at your best friend's brother. You definitely shouldn't kiss him. And there's no way you should end up in his bed along with his packmates. But it's a bit too late for regrets now.

I spend the next little while tidying up downstairs and – as if thinking about my best friend conjures her from thin air – my cell phone starts to ring, when I glance at the screen I find my best friend is calling.

"Happy Christmas, Hollie!" Annie squeals at me down the line when I answer. "I've got the best news."

"Happy Christmas," I squeak back, really hoping the guilt isn't obvious in my voice. "What news?"

"Old Samuel – he has a snow plow, and he heard about the fact you're stuck at the ranch without us on Christmas Day, and he's clearing the path for us. We're nearly home. About five minutes away."

"Five minutes?" I gulp. I wasn't expecting my best friend home today. I was expecting more time to work out in my head what I was going to tell her. To come up with a plan and a story and possibly some self-defense moves in case she decides to attack me.

"So what have you been up to? What have you been doing?"

"What have I been doing?" I repeat.

"Yeah," she says, "while I've been gone."

Panic spirals through my body and my brain completely blanks. The only seriously unhelpful thing that springs to mind is – *your brother, I've been doing your brother.* Not helpful one bit. I squeeze my eyes and try to think of something else.

Think of an excuse. Think of an excuse quickly, Hollie.

But nothing comes to mind. Nothing at all. So I do what

any sensible 30-year-old would do in this situation: I pretend the line has gone dead and hang up the phone. My arms shake as I stare at the screen, which lights up almost immediately and starts buzzing again.

"Shit," I mutter. "Shit, shit, shit, shit, shit."

It's at this moment that the three very hot alphas come strolling inside the house.

"What's wrong?" Clay asks.

"Annie!" I screech, shaking the phone in his direction.

"Why don't you answer it?" Nash says.

"She wants to know what I've been doing since she's been gone. And I can't tell her – not over the phone anyway. Although maybe that might be safer considering she's going to kill me. Ahhhh. What should I do?"

"Give the phone to me," Clay says.

"Oh my God." I clutch it to my chest. "What are you going to do? What are you going to tell her? She's going to hate me. She's going to disown me as her best friend. And it's Christmas too."

"She's not going to disown you, Hollie."

"I've broken Girl Code. Of course she's going to disown me."

Clay ignores my panic, holds out his hand, giving me a stern look – all raised eyebrows and set jaw. He's pretty irresistible that way. I'd do anything he said, including sinking to my knees and sucking on his cock. But I think what he wants right now is my cell phone, so I hand it over. He answers it and brings it up to his ear.

"Hello, Annie. Happy Christmas." Silence. "We brought her back to the cabin. We thought it would be best that she wasn't on her own during the snowstorm."

I can hear Annie's rambling voice from the other end of

the phone. High-pitched, hyper, and real damn fast. That probably means she isn't buying this.

"We'll see you soon," he says, and then he hangs up.

"She knows," I say.

"She doesn't know," Clay says.

"But you're going to tell her, right?" Nash asks.

"Oh God!" I tumble down onto the nearest armchair, bring my knees up to my chest, wrap my arms around my legs, and bury my head in my lap.

"Are you having second thoughts?" Clay asks.

"No," I mutter.

"Regrets?" Tucker asks.

"No."

"Remorse?" Nash asks.

"No. I will tell her. Just not right away. I need time to think about how I'm going to break this news to her. It's Christmas Day and..."

They're all looking at me.

"Don't stand around, staring at me like that," I say. "She's going to be home in five minutes. We need to look natural."

"You're the one curled up in a ball, rocking side to side, sweetheart," Tucker points out unhelpfully.

"You're right," I say. I snap down my legs and lean back in the chair, trying to look natural and relaxed – not like a girl who spent all of her afternoon, evening and night messing around with her best friend's brother and his packmates.

Tucker laughs. "It looks like someone shoved a stick up your backside."

I raise an eyebrow at him because there were no sticks involved last night, but Tucker Parker certainly pressed his finger inside my ass just as I was coming.

"Oh my God, she's going to know, isn't she?" I press my hands to my cheeks; they're probably still glowing manically. And my hair – it probably looks like bed hair. "Son of a nutcracker! Your parents, they're gonna know too, aren't they?"

"Hollie," Clay tells me, "breathe. It's going to be okay."

"No one's a mind reader," Nash adds. "They're not going to know unless we tell them."

But Nash seriously underestimates the powers of best friends and women in general. Because, as my best friend Annie comes bursting through the door, trailing snowy wet footsteps behind her, she takes one look at me waiting for her in the hallway – trying my best to look casual, relaxed, and not like I've spent the evening behaving like some sex goddess – and comes to a skidding halt.

"Something's happened," she says, narrowing her eyes at me.

I gulp. She pulls off her boots, grabs my hand, and yanks me up the steps. Behind us, Mr. J calls out, "Happy Christmas, Hollie!"

"Happy Christmas!" I murmur back.

"Gonna start on that Christmas breakfast."

"We'll be right back," Annie says. "Me and Hollie need to talk first."

She narrows her eyes even more aggressively at me, and I swear my heart's beating so loudly Annie must be able to hear it.

Once we're in the safety of her room with the door securely shut, she rounds on me.

"Out with it," she demands.

"I don't know what you're talking about," I say as nonchalantly as I can muster.

"I know your guilty face, Hollie Bright," she tells me.

"In fact, you may as well have 'guilt' written right across your forehead."

I stare right back.

She narrows her eyes even further.

I keep staring. She stares some more.

I stare. She stares.

And I'm the first to blink.

"Okay. Okay," I admit. "Something happened."

"I knew it," Annie says, stamping her foot. "Did you unwrap your present? Did you knock over the Christmas tree? Did you eat all the Christmas chocolates? Did you–"

"I slept with your brother," I blurt out, because the secret is killing me inside. And actually, I find I can't lie to my best friend.

I scrunch up my eyes, waiting for her to slap me or push me, or strangle me with tinsel. Instead, I'm met with stony silence, and I wonder if that's worse. I peel open my eyes and gaze over at her. She looks – she looks remarkably calm. In fact, there's a smile hovering at the edges of her lips.

"*Just* my brother?" she asks.

"No," I confess very quickly. "NashandTuckertoo."

"Parden me, I didn't quite catch that." She cups her hand to her ear.

"Nash and Tucker too."

"Oh, you little Christmas ho ho ho." Annie slaps her hands together. "I knew this would happen."

I gape at my best friend. "You what?"

"I knew this would happen. I knew you wouldn't be able to resist each other."

I shake my head. Did I hear that right? "What nonsense is this?"

"You're just perfect for one another. You always have

been. I just can't believe it's taken you so long to work it out."

"Annie, don't get excited. We're just dating. It's not like they're claiming me and we're having babies."

"Obviously," she says, winking at me. "That totally isn't going to happen."

"Annie," I say, as the pieces all start to fall into place in my mind. "Did you plan this whole entire thing? Did you invite me here under false pretenses?" I examine her shrewdly. "Have you set me up?"

Annie jumps right at me, flings her arms around my neck, and gives me one of her biggest squeeziest hugs.

"Of course I did, silly!" she mutters into my ear. "Happy Christmas, Hollie Bright!"

Chapter Twenty-Five

H ollie

Six weeks later

All my years of studying and veterinary clinical experience tell me that the reason my heat has shown up two months early could be down to any number of biological reasons. Stress, grief, mixed up contraception. However, my heart tells me something very different indeed.

I'm dating the Silver Creek pack.

Unfortunately, the practicalities of long-distance dating, running a ranch, and working at a veterinary clinic mean that although we speak, video call and message every day, we haven't actually seen each other since that Christmas break.

I think my body has simply had enough. It's decided to do something about the situation. It wants my alphas and it wants them here. Now. And my body knows the best way to get those alphas here as soon as possible, is to do the one thing every alpha can't resist: go into heat.

At first, I'm not convinced by the little niggly symptoms I experience. Fluctuations in my temperature. Unusual aches and pains. Constant irritability. I put it down to working long hours and the countless number of grouchy owners. But when I'm still feeling irritable after a visit with a whole litter of fluffy golden retriever puppies, I realize something's up. I take my temperature and I'm several degrees above the normal base. My heat is coming.

I phoned the pack immediately. Of course, there was no question who I wanted to spend this heat with. But the destination of this heat was.

I wanted to spend it in Silver Creek tucked up in the nest my alphas built in their cabin. But Clay and the others were having none of that. They didn't want me getting on a flight out to Colorado and ending up in a full-blown heat – "heats on a plane" are all very well for romance novels, but the reality – yikes.

Luckily, I have the bestest best friend in the world. One who has wrangled a week off work and has offered to look after the ranch along with Travis, the hot barman, for the next week. I think she's secretly looking forward to playing house with him. And I am secretly, for the first time in my life, looking forward to this heat.

Because this time I'm going to believe what the other omegas, the online forums, and those biological textbooks have told me: that heats with a pack of alphas aren't like solo heats. They're not miserable, painful, wish-your-life-was-ending, ordeals to be endured – they're blissful, euphoric, ecstasy-inducing snatches of heaven.

I check my watch. The alphas' plane landed 45 minutes ago. I've been banned from traveling to the airport to meet them, which is just as well, because even I can smell how sweet my scent has become, plus I'm already sticky with slick and so hot I feel like my blood must be boiling in my veins.

I pace the sitting room, check my store of snacks and goodies I bought in, rearrange the pillows and the cushions in my small nest for the 100th time and then go back to pacing again. My skin feels tight and itchy. There's a pain building behind my pelvic bone. And I'm on the verge of running out of this apartment, flagging down the nearest taxi, and heading straight for the airport, when my buzzer finally rings. I almost weep with relief.

I leap over the sofa, run to the receiver, and stab it with my finger.

"Hello?" I cry.

"Hollie?" says the undeniable deep and sexy voice of Clay Jackson.

In response, I drop the receiver from my hand, leaving it to sway on its cord, and rush out my front door and down the staircase, flinging open the main building doors and ignoring all the pack's instructions about waiting for them in my apartment.

Three alphas stand in the entranceway to the apartment building – all tall, strongly built, and frankly delicious look-ing. One has richly dark hair and dreamy blue eyes. Another has stubble across his strong jaw and mischief in his eyes, and the final has fluffy blonde hair that falls over his glasses.

I leap straight at the nearest alpha, which happens to be Clay. He catches me in his arms and I twine my legs around his waist and my arms around his neck.

"You're here!" I sob in relief. "Finally, you're here!"

The alphas say something in response to my words, but I don't hear it because I'm already burying my face in Clay Jackson's strong neck and I'm taking a deep inhale of his rich chocolatey scent – a scent that has violent shudders rocketing down my spine and my panties wet with slick. Clay squeezes me tight and growls in response, and I lick at his skin – at the point where his neck meets his broad shoulders. Then I press my nose right against his flesh as if I'm trying to sink right into his scent itself.

I think I might be crying. I'm definitely shaking. And so horny I'm grinding my pussy against this alpha right in the entranceway of the apartment where anybody walking past can see us, and anyone coming in and out of the building too. I really don't care. I'm heat-dazed, alpha-drunk, and chocolate-brownie scent intoxicated.

I murmur into his neck, sinking my fingers into the locks of his hair. And then I snap my teeth right into his throat.

"Clay," I groan.

My body shakes even harder and 10 million little explosions happen throughout my body. The man's neck is strong and corded and I only have little omega teeth. I can't bite hard enough to draw blood. But I can still taste his skin in my mouth, and I suck on him desperately.

Clay's body stiffens in my arms and his alpha scent, as well as that of his pack mates', spirals in the air. It's enough to bring me back to my senses. I pull back my head, gasp in horror, and draw my hands to my mouth, meeting Clay's equally startled stare.

"Little Omega," he growls at me, squeezing my ass as he speaks. "Did you just bite me?"

"I–I–I ...."

Fuck, I did just bite him. What the hell was I thinking?

"I'm so sorry," I gasp, trying my best to wriggle from his arms.

He's having none of that, holding me tightly in his embrace, flush up against his hard, warm body.

I hear Tucker chuckle and my gaze is drawn to his.

"You needy feral little thing," he says.

"I couldn't help it," I say, shaking my head. My cheeks are steaming hot. In fact, my whole body is too. And if they don't strip my clothes from me soon and start doing obscenely dirty things to my body, I'm going to have to do it myself.

"You wanted to mark him?" Nash asks me next, drawing my gaze to him where he's studying me through his glasses as if I'm a particularly puzzling book.

I shake my head. "I wanted to claim him. I want to claim all of you."

"You want to claim us?" Nash repeats.

I'm starting to lose my mind and all my senses. My thoughts are fuzzy inside my head. The world is hazy around the edges. My vision is beginning to blur, my hearing to muffle, and everything is distorted. And yet, deep down, in my very soul, I know the truth. I've missed these men so much over the last six weeks. They're all I've been able to think about. That and the life I can imagine we could have. A life together that I think could be darn perfect.

"Yes," I say. "I want to claim you and I want you to claim me."

Clay brushes damp, sticky hair from my face, wipes hot tears from my cheeks, cups my chin, and turns my face until I'm staring right into his eyes.

"Are you serious, Hollie? Or is it just the hormones and the heat talking?"

"Oh, I'm definitely swamped in hormones," I admit. "All I want is to be fucked a million different ways, all the way into next week. But," I add, before he can interrupt, "I'm serious and I know what I want. And I want all of you, and you said back in the cabin at Christmas time that you wanted me too, but I didn't know if that was just Christmas and sex and stuff."

"We were serious," Tucker says. "And the offer still stands, Hollie. We want you to come live with us. We want it more than you could possibly imagine."

I smile. A great big gigantic smile that can probably be seen from outer space.

"Okay," I say. "In that case, claim me, Alphas."

It's hard to remember exactly what happens next, except I must be carried up the stairs, through into my apartment, and thrown down onto the bed in my little nest. Three alphas tower over me.

They said I was feral, but the looks in each of their eyes is practically wild. They're stripping off their clothes, pausing to rip layers from my body too – not that in my hot state I was wearing very much to begin with.

It all takes far too long, and I'm sobbing and squirming and begging by the time the three of them are finally naked in front of me.

"Tell us what you need, Omega," Clay instructs me.

But I'm far too gone for words. Three alphas in my nest, their scents rich in the air, their cocks bobbing in front of my face. I lose all ability to speak. Instead, I'm rolling up onto my hands and knees and, with shaky little movements, crawling towards them. I find the nearest cock, wrap my lips around it, and suck like it's my salvation. The taste of salty pre-cum dissolves into my mouth and I moan. But it's not enough. There's still an aching great need between my thighs. One that needs filling.

And soon that wish comes true. There's an alpha cock in my pussy, another alpha mouth at my breasts, fists in my hair, fingers at my waist, grips on my thighs. I lose myself to the heat, to all reason and thought and logic. And soon it's all just bliss and orgasms that come and come and come, rolling into one another until all I am is a constant state of sexual ecstacy.

Time is meaningless. It's just me and them in the nest. Fucking and fucking and fucking.

There are little momentary breaks where they feed me and cajole me to drink water. There are little snatches of sleep, of soft words, sweet kisses, careful caresses, but they don't last long before I'm mewling, demanding, and insisting again, and the alphas respond, no time at all until we're fucking some more, the air filled with grunts and groans, cries and sighs, moans and whimpers.

It's the most delicious fever. One that stretches on forever. One that has my nest reeking of our scents and sweat and come, that has the bedsheets twisted and ripped and damp; that has our bodies marked and bruised and raw.

And then finally, eventually, after who knows how many days and nights, the fever breaks, the heat fades, and soon I find myself lying in a tangle of alphas, daylight streaming through the edges of the blinds. In the dim, quiet light, I can make out the little mark I made on Clay's shoulder, and I reach out and trace it now, thinking how right it looks in the crease of his shoulder.

I reach up and trail my fingers down my own neck, over my shoulders. There's no mark, no wound, no bite. I roll up to sit and frown.

"You didn't claim me."

The three snoozing alphas stir around me. Tucker yawns loudly and stretches his arms above his head, Nash blinks open his eyes and Clay reaches automatically for me.

"What's that?" he murmurs sleepily.

"You didn't claim me. I asked you to claim me. You said you would claim me. But you didn't!"

"We were waiting," Nash explains.

I can feel tears bubbling in the corners of my eyes. The heat may have faded, but I'm still an emotional and hormonal wreck.

"You decided against it. You don't really want me."

"No," Clay says sternly. "But we wanted to wait until you were in your right mind."

"I was in my right mind. I told you I was in my right mind."

"Sweetheart, you told us a whole heap of frankly deliciously unbelievable stuff during your heat. We wanted to be sure about this."

"Well, the heat's over now," I say. "You can even take my damn temperature to prove it if you want."

It's funny how a couple of days (or actually maybe it was more like four or five days) of being spoiled senseless by three alphas can make you one truly bratty Omega.

"There's no need to take your temperature," Nash tells me. "It's clear in your scent."

"Exactly!"

"Is it really what you want?" Clay says, softly.

I peer down at the three alphas lazing about in my bed. "You know it is," I tell them all.

Clay reaches for my hand and brings my knuckles to his lips; lips that are bruised and swollen from everything we've been doing these last few days. He kisses each of my knuckles tenderly, turns my hand over in his, and presses another kiss to the center of my palm. Then he's pulling me back down to lie among the three of them.

"We've missed you," he says. "Being apart is too difficult, too damn difficult."

I nod. I agree. It's far more difficult than I expected it to be. Far more difficult than it should be among four people who really barely know each other.

"So, if we claim you now, Hollie, then this starts for real. You're ours. You come home with us."

"Yes. Yes," I say. "I'll be yours, you'll be mine, I'll come home."

Clay shakes his head like he can't quite believe this is happening, and Tucker claps his hands together and chuckles. Nash simply smiles at me sweetly.

Clay still has a grip of my hand and he lifts it again to his mouth. He kisses my wrist where the purple veins crisscross under my delicate skin. He inhales my scent, and then he's kissing my forearm, the crease in my elbow, my upper arm, the point of my shoulder.

I'm trembling with anticipation; everything in my body singing. It's almost enough to send me tumbling straight into another heat.

He presses kisses along the delicate bone of my clavicle, and his hands come to rest on my waist, squeezing and gripping me there and pulling me tight and flush against his hard body. His mouth meets the crook between my shoulder and my neck. It's where I'm most sensitive, where my scent is most intense. He inhales deeply. I can hear my scent rushing up his nostrils, I can hear him gulp it down into his throat, and I can hear the sigh that elicits from his lips.

I feel his wet tongue sweep against the fragile skin there, feel his lips kiss me and then .... And then I feel the sharp pinch of his teeth. I call out as they cut through my skin and plunge deep into my flesh, and a wave of ecstasy sweeps through me, making me giddy and pliable and weak in his arms.

We're both still. I can feel his heart beat against my chest. He growls. His arms weave around me, and then he's rolling on top of me, parting my thighs and thrusting his hard cock inside me. I'm no longer in heat and I'm a little sore between my thighs, and yet the feel of him inside me – his teeth sunken into my neck – is something wondrous and indescribable.

His teeth cut even deeper into my throat as he fucks me languidly and I come in his arms, come with his name on my lips, and he's mine now. I've claimed him and he's claimed me. I am his omega and he is my alpha.

He comes too with a grunt, but he doesn't knot me. Instead, he rolls away from me and Tucker's there next.

"Okay, sweetheart," he says, running his fingers over the fresh bite mark Clay's made in my skin.

"Perfect," I tell him.

"We're going to take good care of you, Hollie," he says. "We're going to spend the rest of our days assuring you're happy, making you laugh, and also making you come."

And with that, he's thrusting inside me too.

I know these men intimately now. I understand what turns them on, what drives them forward. I've learned that each one is a little different in the way they feel, in the way they move, in the manner in which they make love to me. Tucker does it with a whole load of swagger, characteristic of the big, joyful cowboy. I can't help but smile up at him when he's fucking me. And there's always a corresponding smile on his own face.

I come quickly, messily, loudly. He doesn't come though. Instead, he kisses me roughly with just as much swagger. And then he's burying his face in the crook of my neck, licking his tongue round the flesh wound in my skin.

He finds a spot next to Clay's.

I hold my breath. I close my eyes. And I cry out another time as his jaw snaps into my skin.

A second claiming bite. This man is mine too. I wrap my arms around him, hold him tight, and I return the gesture, biting him on his broad shoulder. We hold each other, tasting each other's flesh, smelling each other's scents, feeling each other's warm skin. Then he's pulling away from me.

And there's just one more pack mate left. Nash.

I wait for the dirty words that are always forthcoming from this sensitive man, only this time they're altogether sweeter.

"You mean the world to us, Hollie. You're everything we could have wished for and more. And we love you."

A million little fireworks explode inside my chest.

"I love you too," I whisper back. "I love all of you."

I didn't know if I would find love. I didn't know if I could be happy again after losing my mom, after all those dark days and all that sadness. But I have found it – love and happiness – and I have found it in abundance.

Nash gathers me up in his arms, holds me, and for a moment he simply looks at me, studying my face as if he wants to commit me to memory. And then his eyes stray down to the two new claiming bites I have on my neck. He considers them for a time too. And then he lowers his head and bites me.

I definitely never learned about this in all those biology classes I took, was never taught about how it would feel to have three men love me this much, to be claimed by them. Maybe it's all biological – hormones, nerves, reactions, molecules, atoms, forces. Or maybe it's something more magical than that. Because, as the final packmate claims me too, I feel like finally I belong.

Epilogue

H ollie

2 years later

As I step out of the clinic and into the snow, I'm greeted by the sight of my three alphas lounging against Clay's pickup truck like the scrummiest of cowboy buffet choices.

"This is a surprise," I say. "You've all come to pick me up from work?"

Tucker tips his hat at me, steps forward, and drags me toward him, kissing my mouth before saying, "It's Christmas Eve, sweetheart. And we didn't want you getting lost in any snowstorms."

I sigh. "That's a shame. I quite liked the idea of getting lost in a snowstorm, especially if it meant being lost with the three of you."

"There's still hope," he says, pointing at the sky. "You never know when a storm might strike and we might have no choice but to hunker down in the cabin and forgo all the Christmas festivities."

I pinch Tucker's arm. "As lovely as that sounds, you know there is no way in a million jingling jingle bells that Annie is going to let us miss her Christmas Eve soiree. Snow storm or no snow storm."

Clay groans. "I'd much rather just spend Christmas the four of us."

"Don't be a grinch," I say, walking over to him, rising up on my tiptoes, bopping the end of his nose before kissing his mouth. "You love Christmas. In fact ..." I unzip his winter coat and peer inside, finding, as I expected, one of his god-awful Christmas sweaters.

"They get worse every year," I mutter.

"Blame Annie. I think she's on the mission to find me the worst Christmas sweater possible."

I smile at him and then I turn to Nash, walking over to him and kissing him last of all.

"How was your day, Hollie?" he asks, wrapping his arms around me.

"Amazing," I tell him. "I got to meet Mr. Burns new snake." Tucker shudders. "Seriously, I have the best job in the world."

"Still don't know why they made you work on Christmas Eve, though," Clay grumbles.

"Because I volunteered," I point out.

I loved my job back in Rockview, but I love it even more out here in Silver Creek. I know all my patients and all their owners and I also get to spend a serious amount of time with horses. I even have my own horse now. Cloud is officially all mine and I ride her as often as I can. My child-hood self would be squealing with joy. Just one of the many advantages I've encountered since moving in with Clay and his pack and making Silver Creek my permanent home.

"Let's get moving," Clay tells us all. "I'm under strict instructions from Annie not to be late for this Christmas ordeal," he makes a face, "there's going to be carols around the tree."

I clap my hands in excitement. The first Christmas I was here, a snowstorm and all the, well, sexy business, meant I hadn't experienced Jackson Carols Round the Tree. But last year I did and it's one of my new most favorite Christmas traditions.

I hop up into the front seat of the cab. "Actually," I say, "can we make a little detour to the drugstore before we head back to the ranch?"

Three pairs of alpha eyes are on me immediately.

"Is anything wrong?" Nash asks me as Tucker says, "Are you ill?"

"No," I say, telling a little white Christmas lie, "just another gift I need to pick up."

"Okay," Clay tells me, "but be quick." He glances at his watch. "You know Annie will give me such a lecture if we're even a minute late."

"I'll be quick," I promise.

He pulls up outside the drugstore and I jump down from the truck, sprinting inside, locating what I need and trying to ignore the expression on Mrs. Mills' face as she slides my purchase into a paper bag and hands it back. I cradle it close to my chest, climb back in the truck, and then we're rumbling away, back to the ranch.

I think this winter might be even more beautiful than the winter before, and that was probably more beautiful than my first winter here. Everything is sparkling white in the sunshine. And it feels like we're somewhere magical.

Somewhere Christmas miracles could happen every single day. And I'm wondering if they'll be one of our own again this Christmas.

Not that Annie considers what happened two years ago a Christmas miracle. She has made it very clear on more than one occasion that she takes credit for me hooking up with Clay's pack, despite the fact that Clay has also pointed out on numerous occasions that she does not control the weather.

"That's what you think, Clay Jackson," Annie always says, scrunching up her nose and wriggling her fingers.

Maybe my best friend is a witch and does possess magical powers. Or maybe she just saw what me and Clay had been blind to all those years. The attraction between us. This magical connection. The fact that we were made for each other, all four of us

We spent that first six weeks after Christmas doing the long-distance thing. But after our first heat spent together, we realized how much we meant to each other and in the spring – when the days were filled with sunshine and the grass in the ranch was emerald green – I moved to Silver Creek.

A year and three quarters later, I'm still here and happier than ever.

Clay pulls the truck up outside the big house and turns to me in his seat.

"It's not too late," he tells the three of us. "We could fake a stomachache or tell them a fence needs mending urgently."

"Clay Jackson. We are not missing this for the world."

He groans. But I know he secretly loves all this. He loves his family, he loves this ranch, and he loves me. I reach across the space between us, kiss his cheek, and then go to meet Annie, who's waiting for us on the porch, tapping her wristwatch.

"You're late," she says, addressing her complaint at her brother.

"You're always late," he tells her. "If you got rid of that truck and–"

"Don't start," she says, taking my hand and pulling me into the warm embrace of the house.

Mr. and Mrs. J are already inside, a feast spread out on the kitchen table, and so is Travis, the once hot barman who now owns the bar, *The Dirty Boot*, and is running it alongside my best friend.

"Who wants an eggnog?" Mrs. J asks, producing a tray of drinks and shoving them toward us.

"Not me," I say. "I just need to use the bathroom."

I leave my new family laughing and chattering in the kitchen as I sneak upstairs with my package from the drugstore. Once inside the bathroom, I lock the door and pull out the package inside. I've never done one of these tests before. I think I know how they work, but I read the instructions ten times through anyway just in case, and then spend the next few moments trying to work out how exactly I'm going to pee on a stick without peeing on my hand too, all over the floor.

Finally, hovering above the toilet, I find the angle, do the business, and place the test to one side, pulling out my cell phone and starting a timer. The stopwatch is halfway through its countdown when there's a knock on the door.

"You alright in there, sweetheart?" Clay says from the other side. "You've been in there a while."

"Me?" I squeak. "Fine, but..."

I go and unlock the door, finding Clay isn't alone. Tucker and Nash are there too.

"We were worried about you," Nash explains. "We thought maybe something happened at the clinic today or you were feeling sad."

Sometimes the grief about my mom still hits me and knocks me off my feet. But it's happening less often now. And when it does come on, it lasts a lot less time. Not that I've forgotten her, not that I don't miss her, but it's getting easier, especially with these three men in my life. They're one hell of a distraction, one hell of a sexy distraction at that.

There's also times when my job at the vet clinic can be difficult, when an old dog is ill or a horse is hurt. Sometimes I need a hug from my alphas and reminding of all the good things there are in the world. I'm not surprised they've come to check on me.

I usher them inside and lock the door behind them.

"What's going on?" Tucker asks. "If you're feeling needy and greedy little Omega, this might not be the best time, what with Clay's parents right downstairs, but I'm always willing–"

"Nope," I tell him, and point toward the stick resting by the sink.

"What's that?" Tucker says.

But Nash has spotted what it is. "A pregnancy test," he says in wonderment.

All three of them look at me again like they did in the truck.

"You think you're..." Clay starts.

"Maybe, possibly." I stopped my contraception medicine a couple of months ago and I had my heat just over six weeks ago – a heat which featured a hell of a lot of breeding talk – unlocking a kink I never knew I possessed! "There's a good chance I am, especially as my period's late, but you never know."

My phone alarm blares, making all four of us jump.

"Does that mean it's ready?" Clay asks.

I nod my head, all of a sudden more nervous than I've felt in a long time.

"Do you want me to look?" Nash volunteers.

"I'll look."

I stroll back toward the test, pick it up, and stare down at the result. Two blue lines strike across the little window.

"What does it mean?" Tucker says, as the three alphas crowd behind me, peering over my shoulder.

"It means," I say, a smile broadening across my face as tears bubble in my eyes, "we have another Christmas miracle."

*** The End ***

Need another dose of Hannah's Christmas omegaverse?

Check out *In Stockings* — a cheeky omega elf, three hot firemen and unicorns galore!

Also by Hannah Haze

All available on Amazon and Kindle Unlimited.

Paranormal RH romance
The Firestone Academy
Storm of Shadows
Spark of Sorcery
Taste of Thorns
Lure of Lightning

The Arrow Hart Academy
Fractured Fates
Twisted Ties
Shattered Stars
Burdened Bonds
Destined Dawn

Contemporary RH omegaverse
The Rockview Omegaverse
Pack Rivals Part I

Pack Rivals Part II
Pack Choice
Pack Gamble Part I
Pack Gamble Part II
Pack Education Part I
Pack Education Part II
Knot What I Want For Christmas

In With The Pack
    In Deep - Rosie's story
    In Trouble - Connie's story
    In Knots - Alexa's story
    In Doubt - Giorgie's story
    In Control - Sophia's story
    In Stockings (Christmas Novella)

Contemporary MF omegaverse series
    The Alpha Rock Stars
    The Rockstar's Omega
    Rocked by the Alpha
    Fourth Base with the Alpha

Contemporary MF omegaverse standalones
    Oxford Heat
    The Alpha Escort Agency
    Omega's Forbidden Heat

Contemporary MF omegaverse novellas
    The Omega Chase
    Online Heat
    Christmas Heat

225

About the Author

A recovering cynic, Hannah grew up swearing she would never marry. Then in 2001, she met her husband and has been a card-carrying romantic ever since. Despite being an avid writer and reader, Hannah decided to do the sensible thing and study science at university, putting authoring ideas to one side.This all changed when she discovered the joys of a good romance book and came to the realisation that love stories are always the best ones.

She now uses her knowledge of chemical bonds and reactions to ensure her books are full of sparks. In fact the electricity between her characters is sure to set your pulse racing and your heart fluttering.

Hannah loves reading to her three children, including doing all the silly voices, and going for long walks in the countryside (the muddier the better). Her head is always full of new story ideas and you are most likely to find her avoiding the demands of her very naughty cat as she attempts to write them all down.

Sign up to my newsletter:
www.hannahhaze.com/about

Join my reader groups:

https://www.facebook.com/groups/hannahhazehotro
mancereads

https://www.facebook.com/groups/softandsteamy
omegaverse

Visit my website:
www.hannahhaze.com

Catch me on TikTok:
www.tiktok.com/@hannahhaze_author

Acknowledgments

Thank you to all my wonderful readers for continuing to support me and give my stories a chance. Your comments and feedback mean the world to me!

Another massive thank you to my amazing beta reader team — Aimee, Brandy, Courtney, Donna, Jenna, Jess, Leandri, Leslie, Sara and Tara — who read this little story at exceptional speed so that it would be ready in time for Christmas.

Thank you to Christiana for this super cute illustrated cover — I love it so much!

And last but not least a thank you to my family for all their love and support!

www.ingramcontent.com/pod-product-compliance
Lightning Source LLC
Chambersburg PA
CBHW070930190726
48292CB00004B/1174